D0321534

Rosemary Jenkinson was born in Belfast in 1967. She studied Medieval Literature at Durham University and since then has had a variety of jobs including sub-editing a magazine, waitressing in Oklahoma and teaching English in Greece, France, Poland and the Czech Republic. She currently lives in Belfast and works for the Social Security Agency.

CONTEMPORARY PROBLEMS NOS. 53 & 54

CONTEMPORARY PROBLEMS
NOS. 53 & 54

ROSEMARY JENKINSON

LAGAN PRESS
BELFAST
2004

Acknowledgements
'The Experimental Girlfriend' appeared in *Breaking the Skin: An Anthology of New Irish Writing* (Black Mountain Press, 2002); 'Undergrowth' appeared in *Scriptor 4: An Anthology of New Writing* (Green Arrow, 2002); 'The Flame' won the Black Hill Books Short Story Competition 2001; 'The Trouble with Work' appeared in *An Anthology of Northern Short Stories* (Arc Publications, 1998)

Published by
Lagan Press
Unit 11
1A Bryson Street
Belfast BT5 4ES
e-mail: lagan-press@e-books.org.uk
web: www.lagan-press.org.uk

ARTS
COUNCIL
of Northern Ireland

ISBN: 1 904652 09 3
Author: Jenkinson, Rosemary
Title: Contemporary Problems Nos. 53 & 54
Format: Paperback
2004

Cover Photo: Getty Images
Cover Design: December
Set in Garamond
Printed by Easyprint, Belfast

Thanks to Jimmy Maguire for giving me time off work.
The Arts Council of Northern Ireland.
Sinead Morrissey and the Queen's Writers' Group.
Also, love to my family who have always given their support.
And cheers to everyone (they know who they are) who helped
introduce me to a new Belfast and kept me in the pub long past reason.

'Being in a minority, even a minority of one,
did not make you mad.'
—George Orwell, *1984*

CONTENTS

Contemporary Problems
Nos. 53 & 54

'CAN SHE NOT COME TOO?' ASKED my friend, Morag, with a pleading smile.

The casting director must have had bird-like peripheral vision because he didn't look at me. 'No. Sorry. Too twenty-first century a face.'

Morag glanced back at me in sympathy as the chosen people filed over to a desk. Too twenty-first century-looking. I just didn't get it. It didn't make sense. I was directly descended from people who lived in the fourteenth century just like any other person. It wasn't like I'd evolved recently like the computer. I watched Morag chat animatedly to the other prospective fourteenth-century villagers. Maybe she was more waif-like, more medievally spiritual-looking than myself. Or simply she'd presented the right image by heeling out of bed in a rush that morning without brushing her hair properly. She knew the score with BBC Drama, having once had a skulking part in that successful period piece 'Lord Firkin's Privet'.

'This is ridiculous,' I said to a girl beside me who was murmuring discontent. We'd all wanted this job because it was well paid and didn't involve anything more than hanging around, chatting and eating, which was very like being on the dole. 'If I'd known what they'd wanted, I'd have blacked my teeth out and made myself a couple of plasticine warts.'

'Yes,' she agreed. She was very heavily made up. 'What they obviously do is choose the least attractive people, so that the real actors look better next to them.'

We agreed it was the world of drama's loss. As I left the Job Centre, I found myself looking at the other unsuccessful applicants in their trainers and baggy tops and couldn't figure out why they'd been rejected. It only took a small leap of imagination to envisage them dressed in brown sacks.

Too twenty-first century a face. It occurred to me that only two years ago on the eve of the millennium I had actually been ahead of my time. I guessed I should really make the most now of this happy synchronicity in time and appearance.

Anyway, I started to intensely regret not getting the job as an extra about a week later. My mother had come into my room that morning and woken me up. It wasn't easy to wake me up either as I had my head jammed between two pillows that functioned more or less as great white earplugs.

'Bog off,' were my first words because my head, released from its pillow sandwich, knew that it was rightfully due another two hours of sleep.

'Now, now. There's no bogging off about it,' responded my mother sweetly. She always has this nice June Whitfield approach to everything. She kind of soothes you into submission. 'Up you get.'

I staggered into the bathroom and my mother called in, 'And make sure you put on your good navy trousers, won't you?'

'No. I'll put on my naughty blue trousers,' I called back.

'What a girl you are,' said my mum, brimming with cheerful tolerance.

I gritted my teeth, thinking that if my mum hadn't encouraged me to dress up in my ultramodern, twenty-first century suit the previous week I might have got the job as medieval peasant and I wouldn't have been in such an invidious position this morning.

Naturally, I could have persuaded her that there was no need to take this poxy job but my dad was a different matter. He'd set it up. An acquaintance of his owned an electrical shop and one of the assistants had walked out on him the day before, leaving him in the lurch. Now, I would have thought it a pertinent point that the assistant fled without warning, but my dad didn't think it worthy of enquiry and said I'd be round at the shop the next morning.

The trouble was my dad hated me 'languishing on Her Majesty's Benevolent Fund' for more than a week, though I pointed out that at least we were getting a return for all the taxes he'd paid over the years. One of his favourite old saws was 'Once you have a job, it's easier to get a job.' The logic of this defied me. There wasn't much professional similarity between the advertising world and working in an electrical shop, as far as I could see. Except maybe that they both involved bright sparks. Surely it would be better for me to stay home and devote my energies to the time-consuming process of application writing. Already I knew it was too late to suggest this.

I went down to the kitchen for some breakfast. Mum put some bread in the toaster for me. She has to be the only person in existence who makes toast with the crusts cut off.

Dad looked up from his bills. 'All set for the world of work, then?'

'What is that, some new theme park they're starting?' I replied.

'And for God's sake be enthusiastic when you meet the man,' said my dad.

'Of course I will.'

'You need the money. I keep telling you you've got to start working towards a pension. By the time you're of retirement age, they'll have done away with state pensions and then you'll be in Queer Street if you've put nothing aside.'

I try to meet my dad's eyes while he speaks because he gets very irate if he thinks I'm not listening, but this particular morning it was hard to take. 'Come on, Dad. No politics or religion at the breakfast table. Let's talk about something else. Did you read that interesting article in the paper about downshifting yesterday? I thought it was cool. It seems everyone is trying to get out of the rat race and survive on less money.'

'Downshifting?' sniffed my mother sceptically. 'You shouldn't be thinking about that, Ruth. You should be trying to shift up a gear or two. Upshifting, that's what you need,' she added just to make sure we had appreciated the full wit of her wordplay.

And my mother was usually so neutral.

Grayson's was a five minute bus-ride away. It was one of those ancient family businesses tucked down a cobbled side street, next to an antique shop, an art gallery and a homeopath's. You had an idea that even if this business struggled into the next millennium, it would eventually have to submit to its future as a pot pourri shop.

Grayson's was so dark inside, I stumbled over a display of Hoovers, bruising myself extensively. I wouldn't have minded but there were upright lamps everywhere and only about two were switched on. Mrs. Grayson was standing at the counter waiting for me and she didn't look amused at my Norman Wisdom routine. 'Ruth, isn't it?' she said in a tone of voice that implied she wished I weren't.

She showed me around, the order books etc, etc. 'You know how to operate a till, don't you?' she checked, nodding towards it. It was an ancient manual one with massive keys.

'Well, I've only used computerised ones,' I admitted. 'Steam powered, is it? Luckily for you I'm a bit of a retro-enthusiast.'

I meant her to smile but all I got was a quizzical stare.

Next I followed her up the stairs. I couldn't help noticing she had a very fat rear, but luckily she was quite evenly ballasted because she had a very fat stomach as well. First, she showed me the tea-and coffee-making facilities next to the bathroom. Tea making was to be a job exclusive to me. I followed her through to a very smart office full of the latest software. Mr. Grayson was there and he gave us an ursine grunt, a wave of the hand that told us to leave, then twisted in his swivel chair so that he had his back to us. He was on the phone.

Mrs. Grayson had thoughtfully printed me out a job description profile. It went like this:

9a.m. Jobs

1) Switch water heater on (behind door in bathroom)

2) Check milk, tea, coffee, biscuits, washing-up liquid and toilet roll etc.

3) Make sure all cups etc. are washed.

4) Go for paper, milk etc.

5) Hoover shop floor (Friday morning clean bathroom, offices etc.)

After afternoon tea break all cups must be washed ready for the following day.

There was another page behind this going into the minutiae of how to deal with customers.

1) On answering the phone, say, 'Good morning/afternoon. This is Grayson's Electrical Store. How may I help you?'

2) If the repairs on an item have not yet been done, defuse the situation by saying, 'I'm sorry but the part has not yet arrived in the post', or 'I do apologise but we are one electrician short at the moment'.

I'd never imagined that a job could be scripted word for word before.

'If there's anything else I can think of, I'll print another copy out for you,' she said, sitting down by the counter while she checked it.

'Well, it looks to me like you've covered everything,' I ventured. 'It's all-encompassing,' I said, amazed at the breadth of her backside on the stool.

'Yes. I'm sure you'll be fine,' she smiled. 'We'll be happy to have you here for as long as you want.' I'll get my coat then, I felt like saying, but she went on, 'We'd hate to lose you no sooner than we'd trained you up.'

This worried me intensely. I'd thought I was only going to be a two-week stopgap. I was starting to get this powerlessness about my future. How come I'd driven myself into a corner like this? Only two months ago I'd been doing clerical work at an advertising agency in an attempt to get in through the back door, since none of my CVs, no matter how extravagantly I lied, ever got a response. I mean, how hard could it be to make it as a copywriter? The best Fay Weldon could come up with was 'Go to work on an egg', which hardly recharted imaginative zeniths.

Every day at the agency I was waiting for some creative opening— maybe the scenario where a copywriter with mental block staggered into our office begging for help. I already had a brilliant line should he or she be working on a deodorant advertisement: 'Genius is one per cent inspiration and ninety-nine per cent perspiration.' I was so caught up in this daydream that I absent-mindedly sent the already-opened envelopes out with the mail in the post. My boss wasn't pleased when the empty, scraggy envelopes arrived back to the office refranked, a result that expedited my departure from the company.

After my first day's work I met up with Morag. She was pretty much my best friend and a really nice person. Also, I liked having a friend called Morag because every time I said her name to people they would laugh like I'd said something really witty. Having a friend called Morag was a great social icebreaker. Anyway, she was having an easy time out at the medieval village. 'It's not fair,' I told her, 'I studied medieval literature for three years at university and you're the one who got the job. My name was on that job. I was spot on with Northumbrian dialect circa 1300.' It was so annoying that I couldn't use this skill. It wasn't like I could even be an academic, because I wasn't much good at research. The problem had been that I wasn't able to find the medieval section in the library until three weeks before my finals. I'd been given all the reading lists of course but I'd just assumed they were books so old that the library had thrown them out. Most of them had been written pre-1945. It was a real revelation to finally find this tiny room hidden in the bowels of the library but even then you practically needed to don a gas mask before going in the books were so musty. The librarian nearly passed out when she passed a selection through the beeper.

The first few days at Grayson's went slowly. The other shop

assistant who worked with me was called Sina. She said it was boss, tops working at Grayson's because you were never rushed off your feet. If anything that was an understatement as she impersonated a slouching statue on a plinth for most of the day. She was okay to be with, a kind of human equivalent of easy listening music. She did have some moments of liveliness such as when we discussed how attractive she was. One of the first things I noticed about her was that she had a bad case of orange-make-up syndrome—looked like she'd been Tango'ed. She was the only person I'd met who had one of those handbags shaped like a toy sheep. It reminded me of a pyjama case I'd once had.

There were a few initial teething problems in the tea-making department. Mrs. Grayson made a horrible gargoyle face because I'd put too much milk in. And the coffee wasn't an unqualified success either. 'Do I really want to be kept awake for the next twenty-four hours?' snapped Mr. Grayson, pushing the cup away from him. I wanted to tell him that sixteen hours of his waking self was quite enough for the world already. In Mrs. Grayson's favour, she contented herself with making faces but Mr. Grayson really was directly unpleasant. Even the look of him. He had an ascetic look and a face etched with vertical wrinkles, no smiley, horizontal ones.

I had to transfer calls through to his office. It was easy to mistake an internal for an outside line and twice when the phone rang and I picked up the receiver, I cut off the person that Mr. Grayson was already talking to. The second time it happened, he shrieked, 'Put the phone down! Put it down!' like I was a hood pointing a gun at him. Then as I heard him bellow across to his wife, 'This is starting to ... ', I transferred the next call to him, thus giving whomever it was the full effect of his charm. I couldn't tell if I'd done it just because I was rattled by him, but I like to think that in some measure it was deliberate. Afterwards, I wondered how he'd finished the sentence. (It must be the copywriter in me to need to anticipate his line) 'really piss me off'? ... 'get on my wick'? Or could it be simply, 'happen all the time'.

Sina, my anodyne companion, said it was just his way and not to worry about it. But later in the day she made this chance remark about how her father had once run her over in his car as he backed out of the garage, which cast doubts over her as a reliable judge of what constitutes normative behaviour.

The next day I got us both into Mr. Grayson's bad books. An interest in men was about the only thing Sina and I had in common, so we used to talk about them quite a lot. 'Ah, Greek men,' I said, remembering a holiday to the islands. 'You haven't been loved until you've been loved by a Greek.'

She looked dubious. 'I don't think I'd like one of them. I don't like all that business of how they have to have sex with their fathers. It puts me off them.'

'What?'

'You know, that initiation thing. When boys are about fourteen, they have to have sex with their fathers. I'm sure someone told me that.'

I told her she might have heard it of the Ancient Greeks, but she said the young ones did it as well. Then I said I didn't think that kind of behaviour was acceptable of an EU country. Whatever the source, she had a gannet-like ability to swallow anything. She wasn't academic (the only A class she'd ever been involved in was related to drugs) but also she had no idea of what life was like outside this town. I'm sure she thought metropolitan was a type of ice cream.

Anyway, at one point a very good-looking man passed by the shop window, so I got Sina to run out with me so I could show her what I thought was an attractive guy. He was moving at a fair old lick and we'd already crossed the street after him when we heard a loud pounding sound behind us. We looked up and saw Mr. Grayson banging his fist on the upstairs window. 'Just get back. Get back inside!' I lip-read him shout. His spittle flew onto the window like a squirt of Windolene.

'How's life in the electric business?' my father would chirp cheerfully. How could I make him understand that one hour working in that shop was enough to turn anyone to British Gas.

I moped around every night when I came home. My mother told

me to go to the doctor. It wasn't that she thought I was suffering from depression or anything. It was because he was young and good-looking and she thought my life would take off if I could hook myself a professional boyfriend. Not professional boyfriend as in gigolo, as in a boyfriend who had a good career. My mum was regularly on at me for being too scruffy and indifferent to ever attract someone decent and with money, so I had made the cardinal error of trying to prove to her that I was desirable just the way I was and told her all about meeting down at the surgery a new doctor who was darkly handsome in a Daniel Day-Lewis way and how interested he'd seemed. In retrospect this latter conclusion seemed a bit optimistic.

'I really like your tie,' I had said just before leaving, in a classic example of communicating my desire through transference onto a related object. I hadn't had enough bottle to ask him out. I think I felt vulnerable because it wasn't a good start him knowing I had eczema. It's hardly the impression you want to create, especially if he'd planned to have children with unblemished skin. But he did seem genuinely pleased at the tie compliment. And as I'd left, he'd said, 'And any more trouble, come back immediately, okay?' It was like he really wanted me to come back. Like asking me on a date. Or maybe he was thinking he had never seen such a rabid case of eczema in his life.

I told mum not to make an appointment for me. Most likely the reason he had smiled when I complimented his tie was because it reminded him of his girlfriend who had just bought it for him.

I'd been at Grayson's a week, when I was upstairs one mid-morning making the coffee with granular precision for their lordships. The office door was closed which was unusual as I was used to being observed. In fact, it was just as well that the door was closed because the kettle had decided to dispose about a month's worth of limescale into Mr. Grayson's cup and it took me a while to fish the bits out. Then I put in another half-spoonful of sugar to keep him sweet. I knocked and went on in. Mr. Grayson had his head buried deep in his accounts and Mrs. Grayson was wiping her face with her hanky. As I set her coffee down, she kept making high-pitched gasping sounds at the air, funny little hoops of noise that nearly made me spill it. I didn't want to look but her eyes were red and raw with moisture.

I went down and told Sina. She seemed surprised that I didn't know the form. It was perfectly normal for Mr. Grayson to lose the rag and scream and shout at his wife till she cried. Sometimes you could hear terrible thuds upstairs and it was really surprising how many items turned up in the breakages book, written in by Mrs. Grayson's hand. However, the next day it would all be forgotten, so it was best to turn a blind eye.

I felt this state of affairs wasn't easy to adjust to at all. Sometimes at coffee breaks, I felt the tension was unbearable upstairs, but I hadn't known it was this bad. I did feel a newfound sympathy towards Mrs. Grayson, however. She wasn't such a bad old spud at heart and she had a lot to put up with, working in the same room with that man. To show solidarity with her, on the counter one night I left a copy of *New Woman* open at the page which had a feature on 'Office Bullies—How to Assert Yourself'. Actually, I had done the questionnaire myself and was in the 'needing an urgent holiday' category which was worrying.

A couple of days later she called me up to the office while Mr. Grayson was out.

'You know, Ruth, this won't do at all,' she said.

I waited for her to elaborate.

'It's your attitude. Your—there's no other way of saying this— your truculence in everything you do. Your studied insolence.'

'Studied?' I said, startled. I have never studied insolence in my life. It comes entirely naturally to me.

'Yes, both Mr. Grayson and I have noticed it recently.'

'So, you don't like my coffee?' I asked and I knew this sounded petty but I didn't know what to say to her. Maybe she'd taken the article on office bullies personally.

'There you go again,' she sighed. 'Some civility wouldn't go amiss.' Did she say 'servility'? I was thinking. 'I mean, we think you're very capable, but we also think with a more positive, brighter attitude you could help to improve the atmosphere here no end.'

I was stunned. Was I the one who was sitting up here causing arguments and bawling my eyes out? After she unanimously agreed that I should change for the better, I walked back down to the counter dazed.

'You know something,' said Sina, looking closely at my face and for once I just thought she might be about to evince some insight as to what was going on inside me. 'I wish I had a pair of cheekbones,' she said.

'How does your face support itself, then?' I asked wearily.

But suddenly I thought of my twenty-first-century face. I'd almost forgotten about it, but it now seemed a most important fact. There I was, a twenty-first century person, being pressed by Mrs. Grayson into believing that I was the dysfunctional one in this dingy house of medievally dark thoughts. It was more than any modern person could put up with. I knew I'd go positively claustrophobically mad if I stayed at Grayson's much longer. Only the previous day, I had caught myself humming that Madness song, 'House of Fun'. It was essential to redefine myself. Everyone was doing that these days, from nations to individuals. It was time to shift gear into the twenty-first century and leave behind these small shopocrats with their distrust of anyone with an IQ in triple figures. I would get that advertising job no matter what.

Fate has a strange way of pre-empting, as no sooner had I decided to go for a copywriting career than the phone rang and a woman's voice asked for Mr. Grayson. I told her he wasn't in.

'Well, could you find out if he wants the same adverts *The Echo* ran for him last month?'

It was as though a light had lit up inside me.

'That's a coincidence,' I said. 'We were just discussing that this morning and he said he wanted me to work with him on a new advertising campaign. I'll pop round with the new designs later.'

'Great,' said the woman.

'Yes. The old image was a bit stuffy, wasn't it? He says it's time to make electrical goods seem more ... sexy.'

Finlay Lochinvar Young

IT WAS BACK. AS FINLAY LOCHINVAR Young started his first faltering steps of the morning across the wooden floorboards of his studio flat, he knew it was back with a vengeance, with teeth, with big fat FANGS. He could barely move. His legs were wearing braces of concrete and his head was a pillbox on his frail shoulders. It was as much as he could do to get to the phone.

'Hello? Hello? I need an appointment with Dr. Wood today, please. It's urgent.'

'Dr. Wood's fully booked today. Could I inquire what about, please?'

'I need the bloody morning-after pill, what do you think? What happened to patient-doctor confidentiality?'

The receptionist booked him in hastily.

'And the name, please?' she asked.

'Finlay Lochinvar Young. And if you must know I'm locked in the jaws of depression.' He didn't really mind telling her. A therapist had told him it was healthy to share, to download on others. It was like if you had a disease, you should give a little bit to others as you would do a vaccine.

Two hours later, Finlay walked into Dr. Wood's office.

'Ah, Finlay, what can I do for you, again?'

Finlay sat down at the doctor's desk, stretching his arms out in a supplicatory gesture.

'It's back, doctor. The big black cloud is back.' Finlay didn't normally express himself in metaphors but he had a feeling the doctor, being intelligent, got sick of illiterates with complaints like, 'My toes is hurtin somefin wicked.'

'Ah. Not still writing, are you?'

'Yes, Doctor. Compulsively. You know that Hans Christian Andersen story about the little girl who puts on the red shoes and can't stop dancing; well, I have somewhat of a similar problem with a particular black pen of mine.'

'And nothing published, of course.'

'No.'

'Well, I did tell you that the only cure is for you to get a job.'

'The dole unfortunately pedals that same panacea. Oh, the labouring man sleeps the sweetest,' lyricised Finlay. 'Dr. Wood. It's not about what I can do, it's what you can do for me.' Finlay sighed inside. People rarely understood that he was trapped by the elegance of his own name. Finlay Lochinvar Young gutting fish, Finlay Lochinvar Young stacking boxes, Finlay Lochinvar Young driving a mobile burger van ... It just didn't fit. By dint of his name, Finlay Lochinvar Young was destined for a literary career.

'Okay, if you must write, I'm going to refer you to this group,' said Dr. Wood, handing him a pamphlet.

Finlay read it. Poetry Therapy Group. Poetry Therapy Group? Finlay slapped it down on the desk. 'Just scribble me out a prescription for a little benzodiazepine, there's a good doctor, and I won't take up any more of your valuable time. You know, if you'd allow me repeat prescriptions, I wouldn't come round bothering you all the time.'

'Why won't you try the poetry therapy session? It's the newest thing in depression treatment.'

'Why?' spluttered Finlay. 'Because, well, it's an egregious

suggestion. Poetry doesn't fit into my mentalscape whatsoever. Poetry's for potheads. I'm more of a cocaine man myself.'

'Well, it's the poetry or nothing. The NHS cutbacks mean that the expense of your pills is outside our budget.'

Finlay bared his bottom teeth. 'Listen. Give me the pills or the NHS'll have to fork out on some major dental work for you,' he threatened.

'See reason, Finlay,' shrugged the doctor. 'I won't be harried by you.'

Finlay relaxed back in his chair. The fierce approach had once worked wonders on a snivelling Wishaw drug dealer, but he hadn't really expected much effect on a rugby-playing doctor. 'Don't you like to be harried? I like a good hectoring myself,' he teased. And he liked a good rogering, but that was personal.

'So you'll go to the poetry?'

'Yes, but not mornings. I hate mornings. And afternoons come a close second.'

'Don't worry, it's an evening class, taking it into consideration that some people work,' assured the doctor, scribbling down the address.

Finlay leaned forward, confidentially. There was time for one last go. 'Come on, doctor, you know that I'm intelligent enough to abuse drugs without abusing myself. It's the idiots on the street you have to worry about, let's not deceive ourselves.'

Dr. Wood looked up. 'In my experience, the people with the greatest aptitude for self-deception are the ones with the greatest intelligence,' he said gnomically.

Finlay felt vaguely flattered. Dr. Wood, he imagined, would have the most lovely bedside manner.

The poetry therapy class was held in Crompton Tower. It was an autumnal evening as Finlay set out. He'd just read an article on how the trees with the reddest leaves are the ones to have suffered the most from the change between the night frosts and mild days and he was busy threading together a thought about the beauty inherent in suffering. Now he thought about it, the outer extremities of his own

body were beautified by the turmoil of his soul. His hair glinted cupreously. Just like the trees. He wasn't sure that he wanted to be cured at all. Poetry therapy indeed! Why not flower arranging therapy or Tudor monarchy therapy or, indeed, car maintenance therapy? Yes, why not? It was typical of the arrogance of poets to think they could redecorate a person's mental colour scheme by the power of a few words.

L10 was a tiny room with one ancient, sputtering Superser for warmth and a low-watt bulb shining nakedly above the jigsaw of conjoined tables. It reminded Finlay of a nightclub he'd once been to on Orkney.

He took a seat and folded his arms, prepared to be bored. More people filtered in and he observed them with his head and neck held high like a king cobra warning off intruders.

The person in charge, it transpired, was a woman with reams of dark curly hair and large introspective eyes. They had to introduce themselves one by one and tell each other what they did. This put Finlay into immediate mental disarray. He wondered whether to say something along the lines of, 'A person is not defined by what they do, but what they are'. No, that sounded pompous. Improvise. Improvise. 'I'm Finlay Lochinvar Young and I'm a multi-media artist,' he settled upon.

The woman, Bridget, opened a book and began to read. She had a lisp and Finlay found himself unconsciously putting his tongue between his teeth. What a big tongue she must have, he thought, with a frisson of repulsion. The poem she was reading he found utterly uninspiring. 'Believe me, if I started this session suicidal, I came away universicidal,' he would say later to his friends. He recognised two of the lines:

What is this life if full of care
We have no time to stand and stare.

She asked them what it was about. One man ventured that it was about the need to take time out to take away the stress of living. 'And what about the stress of taking time out? Have you thought of that?' Finlay asked but someone else spoke up and his question was relegated to forgotten status. He'd been there five minutes and already he felt disgruntled. Bridget talked about the need to find a quality and balance in one's life and how poetic expression could help to articulate disordered thoughts. She showed them an anthology of her own poems and said it retailed at £6.99 at Waterstone's.

'So, I hope you've all brought poems with you. Let's start with you,' said Bridget, nodding towards a youngish guy with a slick-back. He began reading his poem. It was about love and Finlay thought it was adjectivally muscle-bound. It was an emu that couldn't fly. It was hopelessly compressed into sonnet form like a fat woman crushed into a corset. It stank, it reeked.

'I wrote it just after my mother died,' explained John. 'It helped me with the pain.'

'Thank you, John,' said Bridget. 'What did we all think?'

Finlay stayed diplomatically silent, waiting to see what the others would say. Some middle-aged biddy said she admired it intensely. 'I think John's an excellent poet,' she mused. 'You know, sometimes you just look at someone and you just think, "that person has destiny written on their forehead."'

His forehead is big enough, anyway, thought Finlay, with that greased-back hair.

'Yes, I felt a beauty in it too. He has a way with words,' agreed Bridget.

As long as they're away from me, thought Finlay. He might have known that poor motherless diddums would draw the sympathy vote from everyone.

Next to read was an older guy. He lingered over his words like a panther dripping saliva over its prey.

And my glass curtain fist
Shatters her blissful uncertainty

Bridget made a face as he finished reading. Someone wanted to know what it was about. 'A wife-beater,' said the guy.

'I didn't feel comfortable with this one,' said Bridget.

'Neither did I,' agreed John. 'It's not really at one with millennium feminism, is it?'

'Nineties feminism, actually,' smiled Bridget tolerantly.

'Sorry. Nineties feminism.'

The two were quite quease-making in Finlay's estimation. John was more unctuous than Vaseline. He was the sort that oozed and schmoozed his way into women's knickers, even nineties feminists' knickers.

'I liked it,' affirmed Finlay. 'It expresses strong emotion and that's what we're here for. This is not a lit crit session. It's an outlet for emotions. At least George here's got it out of his system and isn't going home to beat up his wife.'

Out of the corner of his eye he saw George shift nervously, almost guiltily, in his seat and he shut up.

It was the turn of the middle-aged biddy. How loaf-like she was. Mighty White, Finlay decided, would be a good name for her.

'Swan,' she began and Finlay rolled his eyes expecting a melancholy ode to loneliness. What unfolded was quite unanticipated.

'Food,' she hissed. 'Fish. Bread.' She beat her arms up and down. 'Stay away, human,' she threatened sibilantly. 'Fly. Dive.' She faded out with honking sounds in her gullet.

'Next,' called Finlay loudly as she laid down her poem with a dramatic flourish.

'Extraordinary,' murmured Bridget.

'Shame they hadn't been mute swans,' Finlay whispered to the people next to him. They laughed.

Bridget caught the sound of the whisper. 'What did you think, Finlay?' Naturally, she hadn't forgotten his name. No one forgot the name of Finlay Lochinvar Young.

'Execrable.'

There was silence, then Mighty White said, 'I don't know what that means but it sounds a bit like excrement. I was just trying to explore the freedom of the swan ... it isn't trapped all the time.'

'Oh God. Here comes the baring of the soul. Someone stop her,' urged Finlay under his breath.

'Yes. I could feel a positive power in that. And I liked the element of performance,' said Bridget, saving the day.

'Yes, you certainly captured the swan's voice,' echoed John.

'Captured it? Tortured it, I'd say,' whispered Finlay to the appreciative audience on his right. 'More Donald Duck than swan.'

Bridget gave him a sharp glance and said it was break-time. If they wanted coffee and biscuits, they had to put fifty pence in the kitty. One man, Finlay noticed, put an Irish fifty pence in the box. Finlay watched Bridget and John converse in a corner of the room. He was secure in the knowledge that after he had read his poem, Bridget would think him the genius of the class. Because he'd fallen in love with her. Platonically, you understand. As you fall in love with fame. Because Bridget's poems had been published. Maybe if he could prise John off her for a minute, he could have a word with her about contacts.

The Irishman came up beside him. 'You know, I'm a bit nervous about reading my poem. I wrote it the night after my wife left me. Terrible thing, y'know.'

Finlay smiled vaguely. Maybe he had courted success too desperately. What was it now Keats had said about fame?

Make your best vow to her and bid adieu,
Then, if she likes it, she will follow you.

'She didn't go without leaving us a fine Sunday roast in the oven, though. It was pork, no, it was lamb.'

Finlay glanced at him in irritation. He very much minded being bothered by a man who had wide, brown shoes on his feet, like cowpats.

Bridget ushered them all back to the table.

Cowpat Shoes read next, something interminable featuring the howling of the Celtic black dog of depression.

Finlay was thinking the saying was true that everyone had a book in them, but the real tragedy was that each person had about ten thousand poems and short stories in them that they felt they had to share.

'What do you think, Finlay?' asked Bridget.

'At last! I have long awaited this invention. A sedative without chemical side effects.'

'I won't ask you again, young man,' said Bridget. 'We don't need you to bring us all down. There were a lot of good ideas in that poem. It was a very moving piece, I thought.'

'Yes, moving in a way that involves the trajectory of food up the throat,' said Finlay.

'Wait till your turn,' added John smugly. 'Payback time.'

Finlay laughed. That John. He was pretty ugly in profile. His top lip jutted out alarmingly. He was like a fish that had just been hooked in the mouth.

Finlay held his silence throughout the other readings. He felt that Bridget had been unnecessarily hard on him. All he'd been doing was trying to lend a light, insouciant note to proceedings. What the denizens of Depression Land needed was lightness.

Ten minutes later Bridget said, 'Okay, last up is Finlay.'

Finlay smoothed down his navy velvet jacket as he stood up. Everyone looked surprised. 'For the diaphragm,' he explained, placing a hand on the front of his waistcoat. His hair, he was aware, glowed rubiginously from its closer proximity to the light bulb. His face had luminous intensity. He cleared his throat, preparing to affect a wildly uppercrust accent and began:

Simply Everyone's Doing Sheep

Aunt Tilly is quite amazing
In pastures where sheep are grazing
she takes off her kit

straps on her bit
and does some amorous liaising.
'Aunt Tilly,' I demur, 'Some would say it is heinous
to prod prime British mutton with a Tupperware penis
and it rather degrades the ruminant genus.'
'Dear boy,' trills she, 'remember Uncle Raoul?
And his swims in the ovine gene pool?
Yes, I love to make passes
at herbivore asses
With our family it's dyed in the wool.'

Silence abounded. Finlay sat down. Someone laughed. And changed it into a cough.

Suddenly John spoke up. 'It's not poetry.'

'What is it, then?' asked Finlay with lethal calm.

'Poetry is the crystallisation of an extreme emotion or universal experience. This is not poetry.'

There were murmurs of agreement.

'Listen,' said Finlay. 'Even you, with your woefully limited imagination, have to agree that bizarre sex is a universal desire, if not experience. Surely, Bridget, you are above the opinion of these petty poetasters,' he appealed.

'It was clever, I'll grant you, Finlay,' she pronounced slowly. 'But it didn't say anything.'

'Words that don't say anything. Did I just spout thin air or something?' asked Finlay, imitating the facial action of a fish that caused Bridget to let out a deep sigh.

'I beg to differ, O oracle of our generation,' continued Finlay, 'but I do think my "poem" confronted the contemporary phenomenon of sheep shagging.'

'I think we'll finish there,' said Bridget.

'Ignorance is bad but ignorance with an opinion is criminal,' opined Finlay, realising that he'd probably burnt his bridges as far as hopes went of getting Bridget to be his mentor. Burnt his Bridgets.

'And do all remember to bring another poem with you next week when we'll be discussing in greater detail the healing power of poetry,' reminded Bridget, ignoring him.

'I don't think I'll bother coming back next week,' said Mighty White mournfully. 'I think I'll just stick to eating chocolate when I feel bad.'

Finlay caught up with Mighty White at the door. 'You know, I've been rethinking. I was too harsh on you. That poem of yours had a certain style, a certain je ne sais what.' He struggled to express his impressions of it. 'A marvellous disparity between artistic ambition and actual execution.'

'Thank you,' said the woman, discombobulated.

'Can you do any other animals apart from swans?'

'Well, I've never really tried ... '

'You know,' said Finlay, putting his arm around her shoulder. 'We're much better than those phonies back there. We shouldn't dissipate our talent on the likes of them. I don't see why we couldn't go on the road with our own brand of performance poetry. You'd have them rolling in the aisles. Can't you just see it? Can't you just see it?' He drew something in the air with wild swathes of his hand.

It was a brightly lit proscenium faced by rows filled with people.

Mighty White just saw the orchestral manoeuvres of the hand of a madman.

Santa Rides to Town

THE DOLE WERE PUTTING THE HEAT on Giro Bob. Only a couple of weeks before, The Spotlight on Benefit Fraud Campaign (or Snitchers' Charter) had claimed him as its umpteenth victim and he'd been disqualified from his sick benefit. On the evidence of a photograph which showed him carrying a crate into a van, the dole decided that Bob could no longer be said to have a bad back. Bob cursed his luck. He should never have sold them dodgy watches was what it was. One of his many dissatisfied customers who'd threatened to form a lynch mob must have dobbed him in.

After his summary expulsion from the ranks of the invalided, he applied for Jobseeker's Allowance and in the process he found himself subjected to a most extraordinary personal attack by a middle-aged female jobsworth. After a brief foray into his (even briefer) job history, she made the startling accusation that he had no intention of finding a job.

'Like Stalag fuckin ninety-nine in here nowadays,' opined Giro Bob. 'Wait till ah tell yoh superiors aboot this cheek ah'm hevin to endure.' In an attempt at a colluding whisper, he said to her, 'Jist sign the forms, reet, and we'll say nae moh aboot it.'

But the game as he'd known it was over and the woman pursed

her lips, so that she wouldn't have to breathe in any more of his noxious fags-and-alcohol breath, and put his name down for Retraining Week.

In Bob's eyes, going on a Retraining Week was worse than going to jail. The dole had effectually captured him and trussed him up. If he disobeyed them, they would cut him off without a penny. When the lads found out that Giro Bob, the all-time work-dodger, had been collared by the dole, they had a good chuckle at his expense.

On the Monday morning, he turned up with a heavy heart at the College with the other losers. The first class he was shown around was Hairdressing and Beauty and suddenly he saw a silver lining to the dark cloud hanging over him. There could be quite a lark to be had here, he decided.

'D'ye think ye could giv us a shampoo and set on the cheap, like, pet?' he said to an apprentice hairdresser as he passed one of his tobacco-stained hands through his wiry hair.

The girl moved away, looking disgusted.

'Aye, the anely mousse that gans in ma hair is one of the squeakin variety,' he laughed.

While everyone else was watchin a haircutting demonstration, he put on one of the wigs from the practice dummies and sidled back to the girl hairdresser. 'Now will ye giv us one of them shampoo and sets?' he asked, only to have her leave the room this time.

'Look at that baldy bastid,' he exclaimed at one male customer. 'Seen moh hair on a ball in a bowlin alley—'

'Shh,' went everyone and he amused himself for a while using his cigarette lighter to make the wig hair burn and crackle.

Next was a tour of the aromatherapy class.

'Eee, it smells like a tart's boudoir in here!' exclaimed Bob. 'Jist like Madam Pompydour's.'

He was starting to enjoy himself thoroughly. Tonight in the pub he could make a great joke out of it. Someone would be sure to buy him a pint or two on the strength of his tales.

'There are certain pressure points in the body that respond especially to aromatherapic treatment,' some dolled-up bird in a white coat was gannin on.

'There's onny one pressure point ah respond to,' said Giro Bob, bounding onto one of the reclining couches. 'Ye're onny as young as ye feel, so come on and hev a feel. But baby oil's the only thing ye'll need with me, pet. Nane of that otha crap.'

The DSS staff were getting tired of him. 'We appreciate the fact that you may consider retraining in the beauty field undesirable,' said a little stuffed-shirt, 'but under the Equal Opportunities Act we have to show you round every section.'

'See, it's like this, son,' said Giro Bob, pityingly. 'Women are good with a pair of tweezers and men are good with pliers. Full stop. End of story.'

'Well, tomorrow, we'll be touring the gardens. How would gardening suit you as a career?'

'Nae, ah've allus suffered with the hayfever. Nae good foh me.'

By the end of the week, they were glad to see the back of him.

The next Monday, he was back sitting in front of another Mrs. Jobsworth at the Job Centre.

'The report I have in front of me says that you showed no interest in pursuing any career further,' said the woman.

'Listen ye. Ah've given ma pund of flesh to ye and yer schemes. Ah canna help it if nothin stimulated ma interest,' said Bob, reflecting that middle-aged married women were the hardest creatures on God's earth. It must be their husbands and kids that made them so.

'In fact, I'm afraid your general appearance and standards of personal hygiene may be perceived as a lack of willingness to be considered as a serious candidate for employment. We are perfectly within our rights to exercise withdrawal of your Jobseeker's Allowance.'

'Hey, are ye sayin ah smell? Jist cause ah'm au naturelle and divvn't smell like a starched shirt like ye, there's nae need to insult us. Ah wesh ivvry day ah'll hev ye knaw. Even twice a week sometimes ... '

The woman put up her hand to stop the flow of indignation.

'In fact,' continued Giro Bob, 'Ah'm sick of yoh insinuations that ah divvn't want to work. There's nothin ah yearn foh moh than to be a productive member of society, but there's nivvah anythin to apply foh. Tell us whit ye've got on yoh books. Jist tell us, and if there's anythin suitable, ah'll tekk it. That'll show ye,' he said, beckoning her to come up with something to challenge him. 'Come on.'

'That's more like it,' smiled the woman. 'We had something come in this morning that could be right up your street. What about a job as Father Christmas starting tomorrow?'

Giro Bob was too gobsmacked to respond immediately. Inside he let out a long groan at having dropped himself in it.

'Santy Claes? Me?'

'Yes.'

'Is there much work in that line all the year rund?'

'No, of course not,' answered the woman. 'It's seasonal.'

A broad smile spread over Giro Bob's face. There were only just over two weeks to Christmas which wasn't long to bear, then they'd ease the pressure on him a while. He slapped his hand on the table like one who'd struck a good deal. 'Ah'll take it.'

The woman coughed. 'Ah, there is a usual procedure of applying for the job first.'

'Oh, aye, of course, of course,' Bob replied, nodding seriously, then gave a wordly-wise laugh and a tolerant shake of his head. 'Red tape, eh?'

Giro's new job, or rather first job in thirty years, was to accompany his elf on a reindeer and cart full of presents and trot around the middle-class affluent areas of Gateshead doing house visits. He found it very easy and he drank vodka on his rounds so that no one could complain about him. The only problem was that his roll-ups had stained his stick-on beard yellow, but he didn't suppose anyone noticed. When one child finally blurted out that Santa stank, he said it was the smoke from the fires people lit in their chimneys.

His new job was the object of much ribbing at the pub.

'Forst time Scrooge ivvah played Santy Claes.'

'Man, ye're not fat enough foh Santa. Ye're that stooped, ye're shaped like a hockey stick. If ah lifted ye up by the feet, ah could play with ye.'

Finally, it was the night before Christmas. The company Giro worked for decided that Christmas Eve would be the evening to charitably distribute gifts among the children of underprivileged parts of Gateshead.

The cart was stacked high with presents. The elf who was called Brian made a left turn with the reins.

'No, we're gannin doon Bensham Bank,' said Giro Bob.

'Ah thowt it was Sunderland Road,' said the elf, frowning.

'Why nae, man. Them big ears ye've got on's stoppin ye hearin properly.'

'Well, remember to keep jinglin them sleighbells, then.'

'Ah'll slay ye in a minute,' said Giro Bob, taking a long slug of whiskey. He was back on the whiskey now and heading to Bensham.

The cars tooted their horns as they passed the reindeer and cart.

'Fuck off,' shouted Giro, shaking his fist at all the passing headlights. 'Hev ye nivvah seen Santy Claes befoh?'

He shook his head and consoled himself with another draught of whiskey.

'Pressure of fame gettin tee ye?' asked the elf.

'Ah'll fuckin Christmas the bastids befoh the neet's done. Torn to yoh reet here.'

They pulled into Armstrong Street, Giro Bob shaking on the sleighbells ferociously.

It was half past six and the street was full of kids who'd been sent out to play after their tea.

'Back! Back!' yelled Giro at the kids who were clamouring round the cart. 'Ye only git a present if yoh parents pay us three quid! Now run into yoh homes and tell them.'

Some mothers started to come out carrying their purses and paid up. 'Daylight robbery,' most of them were saying.

'It's dark or hadn't ye noticed?' snapped Giro back at them. Aye, and which one of ye bastids sent ma photey to the dole and got me into this crappy job? he said to himself. His revenge in getting them to pay for free presents was oh so sweet.

'Santa, can I have a computah?' tugged a small boy at his coat.

Giro Bob recognised him as the little git who'd done the two fingers at him the other morning. 'Why divvn't ye ask foh an indoor swimmin pool while ye're at it?' he demanded. 'Think ah'm made of money? Ye'll hev to learn that ye divvn't allus get what ye want. But ye'll get what ye deserve soon enough, mark my words, ye will.'

One small girl, however, crept round the back of the cart and swiped a present for herself and ran.

Giro let out a roar and started chasing her.

More kids from neighbouring streets had flocked to the sound of the sleighbells.

Ten year old Kayleigh muscled her way through the throng of younger kids.

'That's a horse, not a reindeer. And there is no such thing as Santy Claes!' she shouted with great conviction, though in later years she would set great store by older men who bought her presents. She gasped as she got a better look at Giro Bob who had given up the chase. 'See, that's not Santy Claes. That's Giro Bob, the one my mam says is an old pissheed.'

The whisper passed along the line of children.

Brian, the elf, sensed the danger and manoeuvred the cart round. In a sudden surge, the kids piled towards the cart, grabbing at the presents. Giro Bob jumped up to his seat, swearing at the kids and Brian slapped the reins against the horse's back. Immediately the cart lurched forward just as a milk bottle smashed against the side of it. Giro felt the sting of a stone against his cheek and with a string of curses began hurling presents indiscriminately at the crowd around him.

The crowd chased as the horse started to gallop out into Saltwell

Road. 'Get him!' they screamed. All the drinkers in The Stirling House had come out to watch and were aligning the pavement.

'Look at that, will ye?' Alex said, bursting into laughter. 'Giro's jist had a football stotted off his heed.'

'Warms ma heart to see the traditional exchange of gifts,' laughed Watto.

The presents came flying back as missiles at Giro's head. The horse's antlers had been knocked skew-whiff. The crowd was sprinting ever faster after the cart.

The sky rained with dolls and trucks, knocking off Giro's hat.

'Fly, Rudolph, fly!' urged on Giro Bob.

Suddenly the horse's hooves rose up into the air. Giro Bob and Brian went flying through the starry night sky.

Then all was darkness.

The Trouble with Work

KEVIN IS A GUY I PICKED up once. Ever since then, he's kept picking me up in his car and giving me lifts. Never tries anything on. Just friendly, I guess. Which is why I feel bad about what happened.

It all starts when Kevin drops me off at the dole office this one morning and I'm awaiting my turn to be interviewed—sitting in a grey chair surveying the grey walls with my feet stretched out on the grey carpet. Sing if you're glad to be grey, I'm thinking.

With the angle of her desk, my interviewer is subtly concealed from view by a large potted plant (it takes a very large tropical plant obviously used to concealing great apes etc.) but you can still hear her voice haranguing the client already being interviewed. I know this interviewer well.

Finally, the client is dismissed and almost staggers off from the verbal mauling he has just received. The interviewer calls out for me and my name rings out around the office. I am well known here.

'So, let's see,' says the interviewer, looking through an impossibly fat bundle of forms. 'You've just been working as a receptionist at a holiday park? What's the story this time?'

She asks this before I have even had time to get comfy in my chair, which incidentally is still warm from the last person who sat in it. They don't call it the hot seat for nothing.

I try to cast my mind back to a few days ago.

'Misuse of company property, so they said.'

'Meaning?' she says.

I pick up a pen from her desk. 'See, I can't help pocketing pens. I don't mean to, but they just end up coming home with me.'

This isn't quite the real reason. I pinched a key out of reception and security caught me throwing a party for my friends in one of the caravans. But I'm not telling her that.

'You were in this job for two weeks. The one before that scarcely lasted longer,' she goes. 'It's starting to look suspiciously like you're inventing excuses to be sacked just because you don't want to work.'

I look at her. She has no lips and no mobility in her mouth. She is like one of those Muppets whose mouths just go up and down. And there is no doubt she is being operated by the government's hand up her backside.

What I want to tell her is that sending me to work is like breaking a butterfly on a wheel. But in my case usually the wheel breaks before I do. I'm what is known as clinically unemployable. I'm part of what they call the slacker generation. Well, I read that in the paper about five years ago, so they probably call it something else now. But I do know I've been caught in society's undertow.

It's like they say. You can't judge a book by all the other books in the bookcase.

'I'm not that bad compared to others,' I tell her. 'I like some jobs. What about that job in the supermarket I lasted nearly six months at?'

'Till you were caught putting extra-cheap price stickers on cans of lager,' she reminds me cynically.

Ah. Didn't know she knew about that one. Comes of living in a piss-pot small town. That was right. There was a bargain basket of slightly damaged and end-of-stock cans and under my aegis, the basket grew to a trolley and all my friends came round and bought them up. Those were great days for parties.

'That's the suborning effect of working for the consumerist society,' I explain.

'Yes,' she says tersely. 'Well, it must be nice for you and your friends to have so much time on your hands to discuss these issues.'

I suddenly get it that she is jealous, really jealous of my leisure time. This personal jealousy does not bode well for the remainder of my interview.

'What about some training? Is there any career you feel you would like to pursue if only you had the qualifications? There are plenty of schemes around to choose from now.'

She shouldn't have mentioned training. I couldn't help myself.

'I don't know,' I say. 'I've always fancied papier mâché classes. Or I tell you what, I'd love to be able to make one of those sausage dogs out of balloons.'

'Now, don't start,' she snaps at me. 'I'm just about sick of your attitude. You know, if I wanted to, I could have you in here for interviews every week. On my say-so all benefits can be withdrawn from you. I can make life very difficult for you if I choose.'

What a power freak she is. She has this big potboiler of a spot she has tried to hide with make-up. It is like all the bitterness in her from having to deal with the people here has siphoned off into this one spot.

'Yes, I can see it's all coming to a head,' I say, staring at the spot.

I get distracted for a second. There is a girl at the front desk throwing a total wobbler over the non-appearance of her giro. It is quite exciting. She kicks a metal wastepaper basket across the floor.

I turn back to my interviewer. Someone has written on the edge of her desk in biro: I'm a dole-wallah (spelt 'waller') and I'm proud of it.

'What about bar work?' she asks.

'You could be on to something there,' I say.

'I mean, have you done it before?'

'Loads of times.'

'Be at Bedhoppers tomorrow at eleven a.m. then, sharp.'

Bedhoppers is the town nightclub. She passes me a piece of paper with details on it.

'Three pound an hour!' I say, outraged. 'I'm not a monkey. I don't work for peanuts.'

I have always wanted to say this line ever since I overheard a businessman use it when he was having his interview. I've been saving it up for a special occasion.

'Forty hours is a hundred and twenty pounds a week. You cannot afford to turn that down or you will be struck from benefit entitlements,' she says.

So there's nothing for it. I wait for her to bash on a few keys on the keyboard at a supersonically slow pace, I sign a few forms and the interview's concluded.

'Hem-hem, Miss Watson,' I hear her voice go, as I leave.

I turn round.

'The pen, please.'

The nightclub took me on immediately. It wasn't a bad place to work. Me and a guy called Michael worked in the cellar bar. It had a bar top about twenty foot long like it was a Wild West saloon. Made a few mistakes at the start with people's orders, the music was cranked up so loud, so people got vodka instead of lager, two curiously similar words under a rave beat. What caused me grief was that whenever I made one of these mistakes, Michael would throw the drink into the slops bucket, because we weren't meant to drink while we worked. What a waste.

Once, I pointed out to Michael that all the big shots in the city would take free trips, meals, drinks, whatever they could get out of their companies because these perks went unwritten with the job and the company turned a blind eye. So I proposed that if a person on fifty grand a year fiddled a slap up meal, well, we'd be entitled to a little free drink on our earnings. I saw the disapproving look on his face and I switched tack to the waste of the western world and starving third worlders. Nothing cut any ice with him.

Another thing I noticed about Michael was that he wasn't keen on showing me how to close up the bar at the end of the night or change the barrels. He liked to do everything himself. The boss, Joe Douglas, the local hardman and crook, loved him.

It was Thursday night and it was busy and it wasn't. Michael was putting a new bottle on the optic and, as I gave someone their change, I noticed this guy with his arm in a sling way down at the other end of the bar. The way he leaned over the counter was very suspicious. I looked away a second, then when I looked back I saw him reach across and swipe a bottle of wine out of the wine rack and slip it into his sling.

I looked at him and he looked at me. It was Kevin! I hardly recognised him out of his car. I was used to seeing his body in a chair shape. The human chair. He grinned at me. I gave him a the-cheek-you've-got stare and a shake of the head. He went back to his table and I watched him take the bottle out of his sling and put it in a bag. How many had he taken? Already, the wine rack was depleted by half.

The stupid bastard. Was he trying to get me the sack? It's all right getting yourself sacked, but being sacked because of one of your dimwit friends is an entirely different matter. I couldn't believe it. He was back up for more, so sure was he that I wouldn't spring him. He responded to my warning stare with a wink. I was suddenly paranoid that the whole bar could see what was going on and that they would think I was in on it.

I was so angry at Kevin for not stopping, for taking me too lightly. That's what made me do it.

I whispered what was going on to Michael.

Michael immediately asked me if I'd stand up and testify in court. No way, I said.

'It's okay, I'll testify,' said Michael eagerly.

You might say he seemed keen on the idea—preternaturally keen you might say—and I thought, oh no, what forces have I set in motion?

'Careful you don't trip over your own feet in haste and break your neck,' I called after him, as he ran up the stairs to tell the bouncers.

As soon as he came back down, I left the cellar bar. I didn't want to be there. I stood by one of the two doors. Two of the bouncers stood watching by the other door. For one excruciating minute I hoped that Kevin would be content with his haul, but then I saw him rise out of his seat and go back towards that favoured end of the bar. One bottle too many. The bouncers ran down for him. Two bounding retrievers after a rabbit. I turned away. Couldn't look. Okay, so the guy had been a limp lettuce, but he didn't deserve this.

The night I'd picked him up, he'd driven me to the golf course and parked. The wind was buffeting through the car, whistling through the undercarriage. 'Like being on a vibrating bed,' he'd said after reclining my seat. He was very quick. I was sort of bemused. Like expecting a four-course meal and having my starter taken away after only a mouthful. 'I have this problem,' he admitted to me. Well, I am no sex guidance counsellor. The reason to have sex in the first place is because it is uncomplicated. The one thing in this world that I have always been sure of being uncomplicated is sex. 'Think of different things, sad things to keep your mind off it,' I said. He tried by thinking about the day he got a scratch on his paintwork. It lasted a little longer and I got to thinking that maybe he'd be better having sex with his car because it's the only 'she' he ever has any deep emotions about—and the adverts do guarantee 'high performance'. So I said we'd just be friends.

The boss, Mr. Douglas, crooked businessman extraordinaire, came down to our bar and slapped Michael on the back. Michael was now the hero, the big man, that rare commodity: a trustworthy employee. He didn't mention to anyone how it was me who spotted the thief. Oh no. Mr. Would-Shop-His-Own-Mother was too busy basking in newfound glory.

I realised that even in one month of working, Michael had so influenced me with his views that I'd been starting to believe that the job was the one important thing. I'd really wanted to keep this job. That was what had made me do it. Made me sacrifice a friend.

I felt disgusted. I poured myself a drink. And another. Then I saw Michael's eyes.

The next night Mr. Douglas fired me.

Another interview was arranged for me at the dole.

So I go in and it's not so bad because the sky's that grey outside, it makes the office seem colourful by comparison.

I look for my usual interviewer but the potted plant's gone and someone quite different is sitting in her seat. Where is she? I have this sudden thought that she has been carried away because we have all become too much for her.

The new interviewer says: 'It didn't work out at Bedhoppers then?'

'No. Didn't suit me. Nightclubs are very immoral places,' I comment, thinking of Michael. 'But, you know, that woman who interviewed me last insisted on me going. She would have sent a nun to work at a brothel just to get her off benefit. I was beginning to think she was on commission.'

The interviewer gives me a hard look, but says nothing. Her fingers are a pink blur on the grey keyboard. She is racing me through the claims procedure. This one mustn't be up for the 'Pressganger of the year' award.

'Give me my fucking giro' is the new graffiti on her desk.

I have this thought of my previous interviewer in a straitjacket like Le Commissionaire out of the Inspector Clouseau films, muttering, 'I hate her, I hate her,' and writing my name on a white wall with the crayon between her toes. It is enough to make my day. I mean, due to her pushing, I could have ended up working in the club for months, years, days even. She was that close to defeating me.

I left the dole office. It made me laugh to find I still had the interviewer's pen in my hand.

And, as for Kevin, he still gives me lifts in his car.

On the Pull

CAN YOU MIND THE TIME A good while back, when me and Watto was deliverin' gear round the country in Richie's van? We used to go all ower, deliverin' stuff to all sorts, but Richie allus saw us alreet. He gave us a few crates of broon to see us through the journey. Drunk? Half the time ah couldn't see the steering wheel, nivvah mind the road. But ah allus say ah drive better wi a drink in us than without. Ah'm like a homing pigeon, no matter if ah've had a gutful.

Anyweys, it was this one particular time ah can mind, when we'd been doon as far as Plymooth, and we were headin' back. We'd not stopped for a rest and Watto, the fat shite, started moanin' like an old, done woman aboot his backache. He said there was noa wey he was sittin' in the van foh the next five oors back hyem. He said we'd have to find a place to kip foh the neet. Normally, we'd just ha crashed oot at the back of the van but it was the depths of winter and we'd ha frizzed to death.

'This'll dee,' says he, forst toon we pull up at. Ya fucker, wasn't it a one hoss toon, a one street wonder. Deadsville, ah thought. It was Shropshite or Staffordshite or one of them places.

We saw a pub, The Hen and Chicks it was called. Thorty quid it cost us foh a room between us. Robbin' Bastids. On the bright side

we still had the bottles of broon to take up to oor room.
Straightaweys, ah phones up wor lass to tell her the situation, like. Ah
thinks ah hears someone there with her but she says it's only the telly.
It's not that ah don't trust her but ah like to keep her on her toes.
Then she starts accusin' us of bein' shacked up with some bord foh
the neet. Don't be soa fuckin' stupid man, ah tells her. Howay and
fuckin' get a life. When ah've put the phone doon, ah think ah meet
as well have a bord foh the neet cos ah'm gan tae get hung for it
whativvah the case.

Aboot half nine, we goes doon to the bar and meets the local lads.
A few gave us lairy looks but the most were friendly. The patter
wasn't up to much. It's funny the things that stick in your heed. Ah
mean memories, not broken bottles and that, in case you're
wonderin, though ah've had a couple of them in ma time. There was
this auld fat boy gannin' on aboot all the fuckin' merits in the ways
of cookin' rabbits, pheasants and venison. Me and Watto kept the
side up with analysis of the cookin' of pork sausages. Ah can mind
this auld boy almost slaverin' at the lips with all this talk aboot meat.
When he goes, the landlord tells us he's got gout and the richest
thing he can eat is chicken. Right enough, the auld fellah had a nose
on him like a purple tomato and the veins on his face looked fit to
bust. Too much indulgence in life you see. Sometimes, ah think
those vegetarians have a point, but then again when a man's coortin',
he must have red meat. It's the protein you see.

Anyweys, two crackin' lookin' girls come in the door and Watto's
diggin' me in the ribs to have a deek at them. There's our rides, says
ah. You can have the one with the two heeds, ah tell him just to let
him knaw ah'm havin' forst choice. Not that he'd care what he got
as lang as it had two legs and a hole. The girls come ower to the bar
and order a couple of half lagers. Quick as a flash, Watto, like a
gentleman, says, ah'll get those. He likes his captures to come cheap.
If they'd ordered two double Bacardis he'd ha kept his hand in his
moth-ridden pocket and no mistake.

'Hello girls,' we say.

'Are ye pair norses?' Watto asks them. He allus asks girls if they're norses. It's the onny female fuckin' occupation ah think he's ivvah heard of.

They shake their heeds.

'You must be in the polis, then. Ah kin tell by yore shoes.'

The girls borst into laughter. Ah've already twigged on that thems studenty sorts.

'It's the fashion, man,' ah tell him, 'Big black shoes is all the rage.'

'Just cos ye read the fashion pages in them women's mags,' says he, trying to mak me look as stupid as him.

Despite of all this, it looks like we're in. We love Geordie accents, they tell us, the soft tarts. They tell us their names, ah don't knaw, Fanny and Delilah, whativvah they were called. Ah'm Alex, ah say.

'Ah'm Clark,' says Watto, the daft bastid.

The girls are fairly on the floor with laughter. They don't knaw if he's serious. They ask, 'What, Gable?'

'No, Clark fuckin' Shoes,' he goes, grinnin' like a Hallowe'en turnip.

'No, honestly,' ah says to the lassies, 'This man may be a dozy bugga, but ah won't hear noot wrang said aboot him. Ah allus say he's like a brotha to us—ah thank fuck ah'm a single child, though!'

Funny enough, though ah hate to admit it, he's not too bad at chattin' to the bords, considerin' that he's the ugliest fucker that ivvah walked this orth. He has these beady little eyes and a big body with a paunch. Ah canna forget the description of him givvin' in court the time he was bein' done foh assault. The man he'd givvin' a hiding to wrote in his statement that he saw a pockmarked, lantern-jawed man starin' through the window into his hoose. Once Watto was free, he went round and give him another good bootin' for callin' him that in front of everyone.

The landlord clears his throat a few times through the next oor, ah notice. Nasty cough that, ah says. Finally, he pipes up—Do you mind not swearing at the bar? Watto and ah say—Right you are, sir. No problem about that. We'll moderate our language in front of the ladies. We allus respect a request of that sort.

'Mind, what a miserable, dower-faced bastid,' growls Watto, 'If it wasn't foh that thirty pund, ah'd fuckin' put him oot the window.'

The girls live far awey and they say they'll need to catch the last bus to get hyem. We tells them not to bother and persuades them to come up to oor room foh more drink.

'We've got a crate of broon ale,' says Watto thinkin' he's encitin' them.

Mr. Sophistikay, that's oor Watto. Meanwhiles, it's last orders and ah ask foh a carry-oot of lager. Ma lass thrusts her hand down the back pocket of ma jeans for a feel. The pair of thems well gone by now. Ye kin tell they're students alreet by the way they can sink the drink. We take them upstairs. Ah'm really gettin' on like a hoose on fire sittin' on the bed chattin' with mine.

After a while, they both need to gan to the toilet.

'Oh, we have an ensuite bathroom,' says Watto, gannin' ower to a door and yankin' the handle so hard the frame shakes.

'Noa, Watto,' ah says. It was one of them connecting doors to another room. Some man who was next door starts shoutin' at us, so we shouts back—Come oot, ya fuckin' radgie and see what you'll get. Ah wouldn't get fuckin' attached to yoh face if ah was you.

While all this is gannin' on, the girls sneak off to the toilet along the corridor.

'That's it. They've done a runner,' says Watto, forgettin' aboot big mooth next door.

'Nah, their coats is still here,' says ah, concentratin' on the burning question. 'Listen, how'll we manage fower people in one room?'

'Well, ya needn't think ah'm ganna stan ootside in the cold while you have forst goes.'

'Me fuckin' neither.'

'Look, they're students, Alex,' says Watto, 'They're up for anything. Who knaws, they might even want to do the old one-two.'

'Well, ah'm not havin' anything that you've shot your jelly up. Ye can forget aboot that.'

'Me fuckin' neither, ye rank bastid.'

'Reet then.'

'Reet then.'

The girls finally come back. Mine steers us into a corner awey from the other two and ah knaw she's got somethin' to say.

'Listen,' she whispers, 'My mate doesn't like your friend at all. She doesn't want to have anything to do with him.'

Now she mentioned it, ah had noticed the body language. Ye'd ha thought the lassie had been aboot tae be chewed in the neck by a rottweiler the wey she kept hor distance from him.

'I'll tell Watto to escort her to hor mutha's, then,' ah said.

'No, she doesn't want to leave me on my own,' said the girl.

These fuckin' lassies, ah was thinkin'. They go to the toilet in twos, but it's gettin' a bit fuckin' ridiculous when ye can't even have a buck with one without the otha bein' there.

I would ha forgotten the whole thing but it was clear she had the horn as much as ah did.

'Tell ye what,' says ah, 'We'll all gan to bed and when they two are asleep, we'll take oor chance then.'

'Right,' she says.

'Hey, Watto!' ah calls ower, 'We better be gettin' to bed cos we've to get back on the long, lonely road again the morrow.'

The big prize cunt gives us a wink as if he thinks we're in on the same plan. Aye, it's to bed for me, he yawns.

'We'll stay fully dressed, though,' my lass says to the other poor wee cow as they both slid under the covers.

That was fine with me. As lang as Watto didn't think ah was gittin' any, he wouldn't be pesterin' his lassie all neet, ah knawed.

'Alreet, ye two can stay dressed, but ah'm takin' ma claes off,' says ah. Secretly, ah didn't want to be fumblin' aboot with zips and buttons later in the neet.

'Ah don't wear undies, so ye two'll ha to avert ya heeds,' ah warns them, 'Mind, ah can't have men's underwear. They're either tight like women's knickers or baggy and shapeless horrible things.'

'Me neither,' says the big, lying shite, pullin' his boxers doon with his jeans in case anyone notices he's fibbin. The big moot reckons he'll have more chance if he's in the buff but he has a friggin' arse on him bigger than a dairy cow.

Ah gits into bed and suddenly oot of naewhere comes this tirrible smell fillin' the room. Ah sits up and sniffs, like. It's like nothing on orth. A million times worse than one of them fancy foreign cheeses. No one in the room's even speakin' cos they're feared of breathin' the foul stuff in. Suddenly ah figures oot what it is.

'Ya hangin, mingin' cunt,' ah says, leppin' across to open the window, 'It's yoh fuckin' feet, ya foul, stinkin' bastid!'

Ah grabs Watto's socks off the floor, only by the tops of them, mind, and hoys them oot the window. He nivvah said much cos he was tryin' to be cool aboot it in front of the lassies but ah'll nivvah forgit the reek frae Watto's feet as lang as ah live.

After this feet business, it's hard not to have a sense of doom aboot hoo the neet'll pan oot. Anyways, we all settle doon in bed again. Ah cuddle up to my lass. Ma balls is as hard as rocks by this time, but it's like fuckin' lyin' next to a body in the morgue. Ah looks ower at Watto and his lass is practly hangin' ower the edge of the bed tae put some distance in between him and her.

There's nothin' for it but to open mair bottles. Ah had to takk so's to put it oot ma mind that ah was lyin' in bed with a beautiful woman.

'Mind that time, Watto, when we stayed in Seahooses with Les?'

'Aye. Ah've nivvah seen anyone as mortal drunk as Les!'

'And you went to take yoh towel into the bathroom to wash in the mornin' and fund that he'd shat in it the neet befoah?'

'Aye, the dirty, fuckin' wee hund. Ah was jist aboot to dry ma face with it.'

'Hey, Watto, ah'd better tell yoh lass aboot the time me and ye had to share a bed at Seahooses. Divvn't get to close to him now, dear, cos the time ah woke up next to him, ah was stickin' to the bed.'

'Ya slaverin' shite!'

'Na, it's true. Ye'd slapped yersel so many times, the bed was like a skatin' rink. Even ma airse hairs were claggin' with the stuff.'

We reminisced like this foh ages. Soon, we didn't care if the lassies were there or not, we were two sheets to the wind. Ah canna recall fallin' asleep.

When ah woke up, the mornin' light was jus creepin' in. Watto was snoring like a sow. Ah couldn't believe ma luck to wake up afore them all. It just shows you that if yoh body thinks its gonna get it, you'll wake up no matter what. Ah starts slippin' ma hands between the legs of ma lassie. She's wearin' a short dress so ah starts to hoist it up round her hips. She wakens and moves, so ah can pull her panties off easier. Ma bollocks are poundin. Ma cock's ready to rive her apart. Then ah have the fuckin' fright of ma life, seein' this arm stretch across me and tap ma lassie on the shoulder. It was her fuckin' friend, wasn't it.

'Wake up,' Watto's lass says to mine, 'The buses start again at a quarter to seven.'

Can ya fuckin' credit it? Ah was so fuckin' near and so fuckin' far. The buses start again at a quatter to seven, she says. Please yersels, ah said. And they did.

They abandoned me to the sweet sounds of the roarin' flaps of skin in Watto's throat.

But ah was glad oor rides fucked off. It just shows that ye should ignore women who travel in pairs. Especially them students who'd gatecrash yoh funeral if they thought there was a free drink to be had. Ye allus git the feelin' students think they're superior but, like us, their world revolves rund drink as sure as the earth revolves arund the sun—or is it the otha way rund? Anyways, it's like ah say ... You should always stick to yoh own kind.

Whatever

OOP NAWTH OR DAHN SAHF?

Which one? Decide on south. Went north for Easter.

I've forty-seven pounds ninety at my disposal—a week's dole. Could go far on that, but I know I'm not going to get a ticket. I have to eat, fill a few curves in my jeans, so I'll take my chance and travel free.

On the southbound platform, there is a girl standing next to me in a short skirt. Two older women are standing a little way off us and are saying, 'Don't so many young girls' legs look terrible in short skirts? Do you remember how awful Fergie's legs were?' The women think they are safe, they think their voices are on a lower notch of volume than they are.

It's time to show support for the one being sniped at. 'Don't hippopotomi look terrible in human clothes?' I say to the girl next to me. The two women see that I am staring at them and they look confused. I don't care. They are what's called the trundlers of life. They just trundle around till they die, pushing round their shopping trolleys full of prejudices.

First southbound train comes.

Doors slide back. Jump on.

All heads look up as I enter the carriage and walk down the narrow catwalk. I studiously check for my seat reservation, rejecting a few as I go.

I think: don't the people in the carriage look funny because the tickets bearing the comment 'RESERVED' seem to be sticking up from the backs of their heads. Typically reserved English people.

See a four-seat table in front of me and a nice-looking guy sitting in the window seat catches my eye. I'm thinking holiday romance. I sit in the seat opposite to him and we connect knees. Sorry. Where's the seat belt? Laugh.

He seems shy, but looks. He likes me.

The train starts. The guy gets up and goes in the direction of the buffet car. He smiles his brief departure at me, to which I give my 'hurry back, honey' smile.

I'm sitting alone at this four-seat table when this girl who's galumphing down the carriage suddenly stops and asks, 'These are free, aren't they?'

'Someone's sitting there,' I say.

'I've been traipsing down the entire train looking for a seat,' she says cheerily, dumping her bag on the table.

There are seats everywhere. You have to sit beside someone but there are seats. Why does she have to victimise me? Is there any need for being so big and breezy? She has a fresh-faced look, like she has just come off the athletics field. She has scuppered my intentions of striking up an intimate conversation with the man when he returns.

I ignore her. Look out the window. She brings a book out of her bag. 'Oh God, Why? A Spiritual Journey through Meaning to Strength' is the happy title and there is one cheesy American guy grinning from the back-cover pic. She pulls out a bag of crisps and devours them, throwing back her head to empty the final crumbs from the packet into her mouth. There's a kind of full-throatedness about the act that seems incongruously sexual.

The guy comes back to his seat, smiles again at me. But he looks disappointed when he sees the girl, or at least I think he is disappointed. He takes out of his brown paper bag a bottle of wine ... and one glass. One glass is very anti-social.

The girl delves into her bag again and brings out the *Christian Scientist Journal*. There's this cross at her neck, illuminated by the sun. Any lust I might have harboured for this man shrinks back like a vampire from the cross. But the man isn't that nice, anyway, I decide. He's wearing a suit. What a little office boy. Also, now I look, he is fat around the jowls which gives him a doleful expression. And he isn't even on the dole!

The girl dips into her big carpet bag once more and I wonder what Christian lust-destroyers she is going to bring out next. The voice of the conductor enters our carriage.

—All tickets and railcards, please.

I don't believe it. It's sod's law that when you have a ticket it won't be checked and vice versa. Get up and leave office boy and vampire-slayer, moving down the train away from the ticket collector. With any luck someone will activate the disabled alarm in the toilets or a drunk will assault the ticket collector before he reaches me.

Some carriages away, the automatic door opens and the air is thick with eye-stinging smoke. There is an immediate change in carriage ethos. The people are louder here and happier. I go to a seat opposite where four Glaswegians-by-the-sound-of-it are playing cards for ten pee. This is more like the holiday atmosphere.

Soon get offered a bottle of export lager by one of them, which I take. One of them moves to a seat beside me. He wears a sleeveless T-shirt and I have to admit he has a body like Adonis, which is unfortunately counteracted by the fact that he has a head like Igor. He works on the rigs. He starts telling me how the company blood tests you for alcohol level and how soon he's going to be chucked out of his job. A tub of nuts is passed to me. I grab a handful even though I get the feeling there are probably four strains of urine in them. He makes some jokes to do with nuts: I'm a nut, I've finally cracked, I've come out of my shell.

I start getting in on the act, just to show him how cruel he's being making someone sit through such abysmal jokes. I say, 'I once knew a nut. Hazel was her name. Her favourite musician was Marc Almond who was more fruit than nut ... ' He starts to get mildly pissed off with me ...

There's a bloke across from me sitting snoring with his head back, mouth open, and I imagine how it would be if a peanut was to hit on the back of his tongue and hurtle down the throat past the fibrillating flaps of skin, whacking them like metal arms on a pinball machine. Just to see, when no one is looking, I throw a peanut. It hits him on the chin and he wakes up. Too many flies in here, mate.

I look out the window. It is high summer—yellow and dusty and pale green. I take a mental note of the view. Holiday snaps.

The ticket collector hits our carriage. He has his cap pulled down over his brow—to hide his neanderthal ridge, no doubt. I shuffle past Igor/Adonis' knees to make my escape. In the next carriage I even contemplate diving into one of those triangular spaces between back-to-back seats where people can put their luggage. No one, I think, would say anything, but it would be embarrassing to be found sitting like a dog in a kennel. I look behind me down the aisle and I can see he's getting closer. As I watch his progress, this manic violin music plays in my head, like when the Wicked Witch is after Dorothy and Toto.

Reach the last carriage. Another four-seater with two guys sitting side by side. I slide into the seat opposite them. Going to have to stay here and get caught. It's the end of the line for me. They have a nasty system of penalties for fare-dodgers like me. I notice that the two guys are American from their accents. One is old and sedate, the other is youngish and demonstrative. I think gay. Definitely a gay couple on tour.

'Where are you headed?' the young one asks me.

'Knobsham-on-the-Beck,' I say. Whenever I meet Americans it is one of my silly little games to say as much rubbish as possible without them catching on. 'The Queen's making an appearance there today, you know.'

'Really? The Queen? Wow!' says the young one. 'We're headed to London ourselves.'

Well, there's a novel destination for you. 'Well, you know what they say. When you've seen London, you've done England.'

They give me a can of lager. They're friendly but I can't relax. I go back out of the carriage and see that the ticket collector is making slow but steady progress two carriages away. About to turn back but I feel two arms fold round my stomach.

It's the young gay guy who it turns out is not so gay. I laugh.

'Who's that old guy you're travelling with?' I ask.

'That's my father-in-law,' he says. 'Listen, why don't we go in the can and fuck like banshees?'

I consider this proposal, but only for a second. It is lucky I am not squeamish about public toilets. I also have a very simple philosophy, which is to go with whatever turns up in life. Whatever is one of my favourite words.

'Whatever,' I say. 'But I have to say that I don't think banshees do fuck. In my experience they wail and drift around incorporeally.'

'Whatever,' he says.

Slide my hands down into his back pockets. 'Let's burn rubber, then.'

'Oh, I haven't got a condom,' says the guy. 'Haven't you got one?'

No, because bringing out a condom is like waiting for the kettle to boil. Also it tends to slip out of your pocket at the most inconvenient times—e.g. when you're at an interview, when you're at your great-aunt's birthday party ...

So what? I decide to do it without. Whatever occurs, I have full confidence that the advancing march of science will have discovered the cure for it.

We go to the toilet. Now I realise why the Americans call it a can. These small metal boxes are very hard to get into without a can-opener. Finally, we work out how to open the door.

Amazingly, it is all clean, white plastic inside, not what you expect at all. Really have to commend British Rail.

We start tearing each other's clothes off and the buttons fly off and spit at the walls. There's not much room, which cramps my style, not to mention other things. I start off in the ostrich position with him from behind and me facing downwards but the train jolts too much and I am in risk of bouncing against the wall and paralysing myself at the neck. We change to the koala bear round the tree position and this is more like it. There's a full length mirror that I can see us in over his shoulder. There's the deep, grinding, shunting noises of the wheels on the tracks, the breathless sighs of the airstreams hitting the metal ... But then, the floor bounds too alarmingly like there is an earthquake below our feet and we go flying. I burn my back on the air-blow hand-dryer. It's crazy, violent, dangerous.

Finally, he's through.

We start putting our clothes on. He says if the train had been travelling vertically, we would now be members of the mile high club.

There is a rap at the door.

—Tickets, please.

I whisper, 'You go, you go' and jam myself up against the wall just left of the door, wishing I would just melt into it.

My American guy sidles out the door with his ticket and I'm saved.

I'm thinking it's been a great summer holiday, even managed a quick romance with a foreigner at the end, but I'm ready to go home now at the next stop.

While I'm busy congratulating myself, I forget the door is unlocked and the father-in-law comes in. He looks shocked to see me standing with half my buttons undone, but recovers himself admirably.

End up going much further than I planned.

A City Loved

FOR MARK IT WAS THE UP and down of the drumlins, the stomach-thrill of their steep falls that showed him how happy he was to be back. And the hills dark around Belfast, transforming by a sudden cloud-shift to the light green of a wind-dried stone. Then through the terraced streets of orange brick where the sun-faded taxis sat parked up on kerbs, the schoolgirls Irish dancing to doorstep radios, the sun running its searchlight rays over every house. Nothing in his street had changed in five years except that on the front window ledges the displays of dried flowers had been replaced by a fad for the frothy romanticism of eighteenth-century figurines.

That was a month or so back and the inner bloom of return had faded and been replaced with a vague sense of foreboding. It wasn't easily explained. Perhaps it was the readjustment after being away for five years. Or the responsibility that came with that because it wasn't the new immigrants coming to Northern Ireland who were changing it, but the people returning after years away. He wasn't shy about telling his old friends how narrow and racist they were. He'd lived in Moss Side for a spell and had mixed with a lot of Afro-Caribbeans. When they'd asked him about Belfast, he'd started on about it being a black hole, then saw their eyes out on stalks. 'No offence, but black means Protestant,' he'd tried to explain, pink with shame.

He understood now that there was no point in locking terrorists up in their homelands, hoping they would change. The only way to reform them was to exile them, send them on the run. And yet, during his time abroad, he had dreamed about returning to his small enclave and belonging. Having seen all the roads of life, he still desired the familiarity of close streets cosseted by hills.

He pulled a clean shirt out of his wardrobe: it had zips instead of buttons. His sister had bought it to try and update his image. In an hour he was going out to meet his new friends. To them he was Mark from Springfield. Funny, he almost even had to introduce himself like that now. Everyone was defined by territory. He remembered how as a child he'd had this image of Protestants and although he'd had the romanticism on his side it could never hope to vie with the self-belief and strength of the Protestants. He had envied them for that. And he'd imagined their Protestant schools, all plain and smelling of polished wood like the inside of a Presbyterian church, with honour-boards etched in gold pronouncing glorious old alumni. Of course, he had never been in one and people had told him since then that all schools were the same. He'd been to the Christian Brothers himself. He used to plague the good student who sat beside him by drawing tricolours and IRA slogans on his files. He hadn't found school so bad but he still remembered his eldest brother's times there. His brother's friend, Frank, had been fucked up, abused by one of the Brothers.

It was getting dark in the small attic room, so Mark turned on the light. There wasn't much sign left of his and Sean's old teenage den. Just some old nails and little circles of white peeled off the wall where the Blu Tak used to be. Old scars from the past, tidemarks on the curtains round the slanted window. From overhead came the stuttering burr of a helicopter, that familiar phuttering like a dying flame. Mark ran his hands over his shaved head and his fingertips prickled. It wasn't surprising he'd been in trouble as a teenager, trapped, coiled up in this

sloping attic room, waiting like a jack-in-the-box to spring out. There
was the time the RUC had got him, hauled him into the back of the
landrover and drove him to the Protestant side, threatening to chuck
him out on the Shankill and shout out, 'Taig!'

He walked to the window and looked out over the roofs, the
chimney stacks like turrets of a fortress. A hundred metres away up
the side of the hill their eroded flags fluttered in the breeze like
skyline washing. He used to stand there as a child and think how
lucky 'They' were. Because on their side, they had the moon, the
stars, one very bright star in particular. It was Venus but it had
looked as bright as the star of Bethlehem. Yes, they even had Jesus on
their side. He shivered suddenly in his light shirt, feeling the
congealed pall of damp cold that the spring night carried in.

Though he couldn't see it from the window, there was a mural
down at the end of his street which said: HISTORY IS WRITTEN BY THE
WINNER. From his time abroad he now knew that was false. Under
these revisionist skies, history was won by the writers.

He'd been across the peace line once in the past month to visit his
new friend, Robert, through the scribbled, gaudy streets. The in-
your-face murals were like two tribes mooning at each other. Since
the Agreement it felt as though the iron curtain had come down with
new people coming in and new confidence growing and yet a
thousand peace lines had been erected, more barricades built up. It
was a tale of two cities—no, a city of two tales. And it scared him
going to the other side with the long legends on low walls curving
away into eternity. The dogs barked at him, smelling his fear or his
Catholic blood and men on white phones stood at their windows
watching him. But there was one placard he'd seen in the
Presbyterian church grounds that lifted his heart and showed him
that old beliefs were on the move: LET US FOLLOW AFTER THINGS
THAT MAKE FOR PEACE.

He went downstairs to the living room. His dad was watching TV.

'Where are you off tonight, then?' his dad asked without taking
his eyes off the screen.

'Just the usual. Stickies' Bar,' Mark lied. He'd lied too through his teenage years before going out to cause trouble. He went into to the kitchen to make himself a quick sandwich. He watched his dad pour another glass of whiskey and he smiled as he noticed there was no top on the bottle. His dad always threw away the cap and sometimes you would find a few behind the sofa when you did the hoovering. Everything in this house always had to be 'all ate up' or 'all drunk', finished to its last crumb or drop. There was no moderation. 'It has to be finished,' his dad would say. After all, something had to be finished as the real business in this city was never finished.

'Got enough money?' asked his dad.

'Aye.' He wanted to say more but couldn't think of anything. Since he'd come home they'd hardly exchanged a word. Sometimes he wondered if he had truly come back to his roots. This barrier. He still felt outside from all he'd known. It was as if he hadn't been able to get home that day a month ago, was still waiting on an isolated stretch somewhere, waiting for a roadblock to be lifted.

'Catch you later,' said Mark.

'Druid an doras,' said his dad. 'Shut the door.'

His dad often slipped into Irish. It was such an unconscious thing within the family that for years Mark had to watch himself when he was out in the city centre in case anyone overheard. He'd grown up constantly having to remind himself of where he was.

Mark closed the front door. He walked along to the Springfield Road and took in the view over the city. He could see the twin cranes of Harland & Wolff down in the far-off smoky air and the towering mast from the police station, topped with cameras. He walked down past the bookies, the chippies, the barbers and the bakers. The shops hadn't changed for years and as a small child he'd always been scared when he'd passed the bakers of the stunted plaster cast figure in the window with the suffering face and painted blue eyes worthy of a Madonna, topped by a chef's hat. It had always given him the creeps and it was still standing there in its anachronistic splendour.

He turned into the Falls. He passed a group of men coming out of the pub. He knew them individually but could see that each of their faces had the pinched fixedness of heroes or brutes. It was all the same. You took on the appearance of what you wanted to be in life. But he knew the subtle rebellion had already started as, like him, they had shaven heads, almost in contravention of the idealised image of the wiry-haired Irish youth who stared down at them out of the walls.

He passed a mural, fresh-sprouted that very day from organic hatred, which said: REJECT THE NEW RUC. It made him uncomfortable, as if Big Brother were watching, making you toe the party line, issuing community directives that you had to obey. He knew it was all a lie. The upper echelons decreed that the police force had to be Protestant to add grist to their own mill. You will only be happy in a United Ireland, they said. It was like the promise of eternal life by the Church. And he didn't even dare let his own father see that he'd got a British passport, not an Irish passport, because the Irish passport cost thirty pounds more. And the whole joke was that England was no different from here except that maybe here they dreamed more, saw more visions in the mist of the Irish rain.

He caught the bus into the centre of town, passing the packed restaurants lit up by the ultra-fashionable ultraviolet lights, each window bearing the fiery sunflower faces of people drunk on wine and good food. Stencilled on the pavements in chalk was the Guinness message: BELIEVE IN YOURSELF, with a harp representing the letter V.

From Donegall Place he got another bus to East Belfast and after the bright centre, the streets sank into semi-darkness again, the churches shrouded in the dimmest of lights, not wanting to draw attention to themselves. He remembered hearing of a gang over this side of town who lay in wait for Catholics with hammers. He wondered if it were apocryphal or true. Whatever the case, you could freak yourself out by dwelling on it. He reminded himself of some verse of John his mother had told him as a child when he was afraid of monsters in the dark. When John asked Jesus why he wasn't scared of going back to Judea where the Jews had tried to stone him to death, He answered simply, 'Only at night is there danger of a wrong step because of the dark.' Surely there was nothing to fear at night but the hollows in the pavement.

By the time he got off the bus, it began to pour, the wind lashing up fronds of rain that stung his face; he could hardly find where the pub was.

He pushed himself through the murky doorwell into a room of dark-wood nooks and booths. You could smell the damp coats and hair like retted flax exuding the smoke of cigarettes. The men at the bar looked at him as they drank, wiping Guinness off their lips like a secret whisper. What was it people said when they joked about pubs in East Belfast? If you don't come with a gun, they give you one at the door.

Thankfully, Robert was heading towards him, holding out his hand in welcome.

Robert shepherded him over to a table of his friends, introducing him as Mark from Springfield.

'Nice night,' he said, wiping the rain from his eyes.

'Don't you love the rain? Sure, you make beer from rain,' said one of the boys, Wesley, with a grin, revealing teeth spaced out and broken like a Neolithic stone ring.

'Sharp shirt,' said Robert, tapping Mark on the chest.

'My sister bought it for me,' said Mark, looking down, noticing how soaked it was.

'He looks like a wet snotter to me,' laughed Wesley. Mark laughed too. Harsh Ulster sarcasm was an outlet for the inner violence, a tap cracked into a wooden barrel.

The glass collector marched past their table, glasses stacked up straight against his left shoulder like he was holding a rifle.

'Mark here's been living away for years, haven't you?' said Robert.

And so Mark started telling them all about the countries he'd been to in Europe. He'd been in Poland and proved it by his grasp of swearwords. 'Kurva match,' he taught them. He said it meant motherfucker but he wasn't even sure of that. It didn't matter.

Swearwords were like free souvenirs to bring back and give to your friends. Then he started telling everyone how abroad had changed him. They all listened, even Wesley, who said sarcastically at first, 'Tell us a story.'

Wesley had been one of the worst. He'd made petrol bombs, pipe bombs, he'd burnt down a chapel, he'd sold drugs, he'd nearly brained an old man with a brick.

'But I don't care any more what anyone is,' he opened up to Mark. 'I'm a humanitarian; I like people's company.'

Mark started to relax in the busy pub; the beer was flowing. They hardly heard when a few hours later the landlord brayed, 'Get off your asses and give us your glasses.'

Mark shivered as he felt a cold draught coming in from the open door.

'Druid an doras,' he called.

An icy silence descended, that cold knife that he'd always dreaded sliced into his chest. What had he said?

'Irish,' someone uttered from metres away. A man slammed his glass down like a gauntlet.

The landlord was staring at them.

Wesley punched Mark on the shoulder.

'Aye, it's Gaelic,' Wesley answered sharply. 'Didn't that champion of Ulster, Cúchulain, speak Gaelic? Tiocfaidh ar la!' he shouted. 'Our day will come. Whatever we are.'

Silence, like a fork in a road. Wesley shouted the words again.

'Tiocfaidh ar la!' returned some men at the bar, raising their glasses.

'Thank you,' Mark said to Wesley. He was almost crying with relief.

'No problem,' grinned Wesley. 'You see, Irish belongs to us all.'

Mark felt a weight fly up from his shoulders. The final roadblock had been lifted.

Body Beautiful

THERE WERE NEVER MANY CUSTOMERS IN the lingerie shop, mainly browsers who would check the tag, then puff out their cheeks to show they were blown away by the price. Fleur and the shop owner, Liz, gave most of their attention to the regulars: the prostitutes who came for the baby-doll negligees and fur-trimmed slips; the tall, slim professionals who came in for their little padded miracles; the housewives trying to pep up their bedroom image. The shop was illusory world while outside it was January and everyone was covered up.

Nine in the morning and the frost was misting off the roofs and steaming above the trees in haloes warmed by the low sun. Workers were walking fast, snores still in their nostrils, spuming out a great mist of handlebar whiskers.

A girl came in with her mother followed by a train of strong perfume. They were looking for bridal wear and Fleur scented an easy sale, knowing that brides only ever wanted the best, once, of course, they'd compromised on choosing a husband.

Just then, through the window, Fleur saw him: the homeless man walking on his zimmer frame, legs bandaged up under his joggers, his trainers unlaced, the flaps pulled down. He often took a rest at the bus stop near the shop. Fleur had spoken to him a few times, without shoving money into his hand, making a donation in humanity instead by listening to his story. He'd been in hospital two months with his legs when the Housing Exec had put up a steel door and steel bars on his house because of vandals. Now he had to live in the Sandy Row homeless hostel.

'I'm on my motorbike,' he'd said with a laugh, patting the zimmer. 'This here one's my second. I wore the rubber stoppers down to the aluminium, I used it that much. I'm fifty-seven and I was never ill till this year. Ulcer in the gullet and now this. Ah, well. It was cold yesterday,' he said, a cold tear rolling down his cheek. Sitting, can of lager in hand. 'Don't like pubs,' he said robustly. 'Too many bad folk, you don't know what you're getting into.'

Maybe his legs would never get better because he wouldn't rest, he had too much get up and go. He was born and bred on the Lisburn Road, which was strange because he occupied this street, owned it with his presence more than the property owners themselves. While she would bring him news of the impending war with Iraq, he was able to tell her which of the well-heeled people walking past had partners who had hit the drink.

Fleur wanted to speak to him but the bride needed moral support now, having manoeuvred herself into a white body bone-lined for holding the form. Behind the red curtain of the changing room, Fleur surveyed her looking crushed and faint, 'less Jean-Paul Gaultier and more like a toothpaste tube squeezed in the middle', as Liz would have said. She assured the bride's mother that this body-line would make the wedding dress.

Fifty-seven he was, she kept thinking. Her father, had he lived, would have been the same age. Recently, she'd bumped into a woman who used to be a cleaner at her father's old office. 'Ach, he was a decent man,' the woman had reminisced. 'A kind body. Always had time for you.' At home, Fleur had begun searching for his face in old photos.

She doubted somehow that her parents would have found one

another had they been on the single scene now. She'd wandered through various relationships herself. In her experience most men were drawn by her soft, unblemished face and gentle accent into thinking she was light-heared and malleable. 'You're so relaxed,' people would say, judging her by her body, and yet she was nervous and seething underneath.

She'd been six when her father had died of a heart attack. Only last week, a friend had mentioned the irony of Bernadette McAliskey being rushed into the Royal all those years ago and taking the bed of a senior police officer who had just died from gunshot wounds. It had suddenly panicked her to think of someone taking her father's bed moments after he'd died.

As soon as the customers had left, she made some excuse to Liz and ran out. She checked the surrounding streets: on the right, old terraces hirpling down to the foot of the bone-yellow Belfast hills floured with snow; on the left, leafy town-houses and beechnut spires, but he had already gone.

When she did meet him again, he was walking up from Sandy Row, the clouds closing in on the sun in spiralling shutters. A tear again was leaking from his weather-bleached face. She remarked on his haircut.

'The same old boy has cut it this forty years. He's eighty odd and near blind but he still makes a decent fist of it. I'm just happy with a couple of wee nicks. As long as I keep my ears.'

He laughed through cropped teeth and his red-cherry tongue popped out as it changed into a cough. There wasn't a lot of emotion in his face; apart from the occasional smile, it was always in repose. The women who came to the shop paid hundreds in Botox injections for the same effect.

'Where do you live?' It was a question he had asked on every occasion. 'Oh, I know it. I put all the plumbing in on that street before I was F.U.C.K.E.D.' He looked down at his legs.

She thought of the irony of the man helping to build houses. His jacket was buffeting noisily under fractious skies.

He sucked in his lips as if sipping hot soup. 'Boys, but it's cold pushing this metal and me after losing a glove. Would you believe it, six times I lost one of these gloves and each time it came back. The taxi drivers pick them up for us.'

It gave him pleasure that people cared about his tatty few possessions. She understood it wasn't important how much you owned. It mattered more if one thing you owned gave an opportunity to people to practice kindness.

Back at the shop, the silk suddenly felt like sandpaper full of static, snagged on her fingers, made her squirm like silver foil on fillings, wool on eczema. She remembered the anti-war protestor with red megaphone lips blasting out her opinions in the city centre, the volunteers from the Whitewell Tabernacle on busy Friday nights on Botanic thrusting tracts at you, but the only person she wanted to listen to was this man. It wasn't that he had any great wisdom to impart. It was enough that he led his life in the simplicity of a parable, that he exercised his own freedom with energy, overcoming his broken-down body. His spirit far outweighed his body.

Friday night, she went to Bracken's with her friend, Solenne. Bracken's was a.k.a. Felon's, a who's who of hunger strikers who'd bought the place out and now wore expensive suits, but she liked watching the Celtic bands, the flutes black as Guinness and violins varnished to the rich amber of Bushmills.

Solenne had the swarthy complexion and dark eyes of her native Southern France and she was spending a year in Belfast as French assistant at St. Jude's. Her face was attractive but cramped, maybe a little too short on room to hold her strong features, as though her overpowering nature had outgrown her delicate size. Men found her hot.

She and Fleur were downing shots like it was rocket fuel, injecting their personalities into the bar. Two men were immediately attracted, only in their early twenties but very good-looking.

'This woman can teach you everything about life,' Solenne was saying to one of them with a wink at Fleur as though they were conspirators.

'Great! When do we start?' asked the boy eagerly.

'Monday morning lessons start,' said Fleur, trying to hold on to the lightness.

Solenne tutted. She took her aside urgently. 'No, tonight. Don't you miss flesh on flesh? Look, I want a sex toy but I don't think I'm ready for it. I think you are. Are you agreeable?' She reverted to French, as the boy was trying to listen in. 'See, he has a dirty look in his eyes. Coquin. The other one is a slut but this one is good for you, I am certain.'

'J'ai mal à la tête blah blah,' the boy was laughing with his friend. 'It's not fair of you two to speak in French.'

The hand shadow-fluttered behind the bodhran. The boy's brown eyes were shining expectantly. He was turning his glass round and round in the light, nervous-fingered. He was so handsome, his hair tousled with gel, the black lycra shirt tight across his chest; he reminded her of the clean-cut boys she'd known at college, who came from nice homes. She was scared suddenly of playing with him.

Solenne turned to the boy. 'Don't get excited. She says no.'

Once the deal hadn't been struck, the beautiful fragility of possibilities disappeared, the alcohol died, even the boy's looks faded. The boy switched his attentions to Solenne.

'What's the betting he doesn't have any luck with her either?' said his friend putting out his hand for Fleur to accept the bet.

She left as soon as the band had finished in spite of Solenne's protests. A fine sleet was blowing hard like the white buzzing static against the black backdrop of old Pathé newsreels. The winds had soaked and peeled the posters off their hoardings, leaving them in tatters. She walked through the slush and mulched takeaway wrappers till she was halfway home before stopping, confused, longing to go back for the boy but knowing the bar would be closed. Then she began to shake and batter herself with her own regret.

He was sitting on one of the orange plastic chairs in the Co-op entrance, taking refuge from the freezing winds. Outside, night was ploughing in behind raw pink tracks in the sky. When she said hello, this time it took a while before the recognition came.

'They put on Christmas dinner for us at the hostel. It was all out of a packet. Party hats? No, they didn't go that far. I prefer to eat out anyway.'

'Yeah, Italian, Chinese, Indian ... ' As soon as she said it she felt guilty for teasing him. She suddenly smelt the urine, noticed the stains that had seeped through his joggers. He was wearing a cap. A bitter-sweet memory came into her head of the teacher asking them to draw a picture of their parents. She had drawn one of the man who cut their hedges and put her father's cap on him.

He began talking of his own son and daughter in England.

'I lost their address in 1997 in a fire. But it wasn't a chip pan or a fag that started it, like they said. It was electrical.'

He looked at her distrustfully for a moment as though she could be a member of 'they'.

She opened her shopping bags.

'Don't be giving me sweets, now. Aye, I'll have an orange.'

He put the orange into his pocket and a crumpled beer can fell out onto the floor. She swooped on it and went to put it in the bin.

'No, put it in the one outside. They don't like you drinking in here.'

She was embarrassed for him, so she said goodnight and hurried out to the car park where frozen sleet sparkled on car windscreens in an illusion of shattered glass.

A large woman with a prolapsed chest, resembling a landslide in its bally wool sweater, left the shop and Liz rolled her eyes.

'It's not my fault we had nothing that fitted. God, Fleur, you'd need a bloody engineering degree to help her. It's not a bra she needs, it's a pair of cranes.'

Fleur smiled. Whenever Liz spoke, no matter how sarcy her comments, she would use her hands sloping downwards from the wrist, palms facing up and lightly cupped, in the aspect of a saint. Spiritual hands, Fleur thought.

Her own customer was in the changing room and she could see her slim silhouette through the brightly lit red curtain. She watched her turn in profile to face the mirror, flicking her hair back from her shoulders, touching the skin above her chest, smoothing down her stomach. Fleur stood, staring, plucking her thumbnail agitatedly on the white ceramic notes of her teeth. She was consumed by aching thoughts of the boy, haunted by flashbacks that never happened, a constant revisionism that told her she must have brought him back that night for a private party. Must have, could have, should have—didn't ...

On Sunday, she went to church and took Communion. She stood in line and received the bread in her cupped hands. As she placed it into her mouth, she saw not Christ's body but a body of a fit twenty-year-old, muscular and smooth.

Christ, what's happening, she cried to herself. I need it. I'm human. Please help me, God. I should have ... If I had, it would have fucked off by now, the longing. Self-denial. It's no good for you. He was so beautiful. Oh, I know, I know. You cannot be drinking the cup of Jehovah and the cup of demons. Corinthians, what chapter, oh never mind. The pain. Lord, please stop this feeling.

Nothing worked over the next days. There was too much time to think in the shop. She blurred the nights with alcohol and marijuana, rubbing her forehead, rippling the skin into great waves. When she opened her eyes in the morning she closed them again with her fingers as one shut the eyes of the dead. Each day the horizon lay fortressed with a grey peace wall of clouds. She saw herself lying in a coffin with the bump of pregnancy suddenly hatching out into an explosion of dry lace. And she thought of the homeless man wrapped in bandages to the tops of his thighs, heard him crying out to her that there was no sex in the next world.

It might have made her feel better picking up any beautiful younger man but the problem was she craved the loving, shining eyes the most. It still took her breath away how he had looked at her. She didn't know why she was beating herself up with her obsession. She could still try to find the boy as she remembered him mention that he worked for an estate agent on the Lisburn Road. Oh, it was stupid, she knew, but she asked Liz for an hour off work and headed out, deciding she would go into every estate agent's under the guise of asking about property.

The wind was sweeping across the streets, the trees standing like tight broomsticks. The roof slates were a wet mauve under the blueing sky, drying pale grey in the wind, reflecting the constant sky-change. She moved quickly, the speed of her steps masking the indecision in her mind. She half-hoped she wouldn't see him but the point of it was now a rail against fate.

Ahead of her, on the other side of the street a crowd had gathered. She saw a glint of aluminium twisted on the road and her heart vaulted a beat as she ran over. Within a ring of bystanders the homeless man was stretched out unconscious. His jumper had gathered up on his chest, revealing what she thought was a torn vest. With a gasp she realised it was the white powdered perfection of his skin deep-gashed and grazed.

The crowd hushed in shame as a famished greyhound trotted forward and put its quivering head out to sniff the man. An angry shout pulled the dog back. A man was gesturing to the police, punching his fist into his hand to show the impact of vehicle against body. She caught words muttered from behind like 'on the piss' and 'blocked' and 'wallocksed' but when she turned, all the faces were stony and immersed in a kind of epitaph contemplation.

The ambulance crew hunkered down and placed a mask over his mouth and nose. He was stretchered into the ambulance, his arm dangling, the thumb and forefinger, both dark as a burnt loaf, closed together as though he was holding onto something infinitesimally small. The crowd dispersed, blown away by the wind. She suddenly felt something spongy underfoot and saw with a rush of pain and tenderness it was his glove. She would keep it for him. But in the space where he'd been lying, blood was slowly circuiting the small paving stones, like an angry rune prophesying a death.

She walked slowly back to the shop. Liz was too busy to notice what was wrong and disappeared into the storeroom. Fleur gently extracted a bra from a hanger and placed one of the deep white cups over her face, taking breath after warm breath, finding an image of her father in her mind and letting go.

Taking Care of Business

ON A HOT SUNDAY EVENING IN August, Sandy Row was hiving. Youths were hanging round the street corners in groups, fists in the pockets of their hooded shirts, still clenched from the previous night's riots. They yawned from sleeping all day. Outside the Royal, a group of men, golded-up in their chains, were drinking carry-outs, using the bin as a table. Nearby, children as young as ten were swigging from a bottle behind a knocked-down wall that still bore vestiges of an old UVF mural.

Two youths hurried past the Royal and past Buzzin Badger's. One of the youths, Hoey, looked in and waved briskly to Badger who was chatting at the counter. Hoey had a white plaster on his upper arm covering the tattoo Badger had done for him. Originally, he'd toyed with the idea of getting a British bulldog but with all the anti-British sentiment flying around now, he'd decided to go for the pitbull.

His friend, Merv, a pockmarked nineteen-year-old, checked himself out in the mirrors without interrupting his step. That afternoon a hairdresser had shaved the sides and the back of his head, leaving a neat conflagration of golden-blond hair on top. He was well-groomed but he'd never be as popular with the girls as Hoey who had dark hair gelled at front into a wild thicket, hazel-flecked blue eyes and white skin.

They passed the blue shop front of The Ulster Society. Merv attended a class there on a Tuesday night to learn about politics and the art of debating. Hoey had told him many times he was a gimp for joining and it was a take-on, just a way of trying to keep people off the streets, giving them false hopes that would never come to anything.

They were about to cross a side street when a taxi pulled round. It braked suddenly and a tourist, her torso emerging from the open window, took a quick photo of them against the mural backdrop. Before they could think of anything to say, the woman retracted her long periscope body inside the taxi and the driver sped off. They stood a second, feeling somewhat violated like stars snapped by the paparazzi, yet at the same time, they couldn't help but be flattered.

'Come on,' said Hoey.

The two veered off left. The eye-in-the-sky grumbled ever louder and Merv glanced upwards, then spat on the pavement.

Not far away in Schomberg Street, Pat McKelvey turned up the sound on her television. When that had no effect on drowning out the helicopter, she got up and closed the window. The picture began to flicker—drat it! There was never such a problem in Southampton.

She hadn't meant to stay here so long. It had been two weeks since her brother's funeral but she'd become embroiled in the selling of his house and belongings. It had taken days to cart the things down from the attic and put the ads in the paper. What would have happened if she hadn't been granted permission to come over?—the whole of the family in England and not one of them willing to put a foot back here again. Fair enough, her brother, Brian, had offered to do it but only very reluctantly. She had turned him down as if trying to do the right thing by him when really, if she had admitted it to herself, it was about the longing in her to see her birthplace one last time. And it had done her good in the first days here to see the easy wave of hands across the road, the friendly toot of cars and the crack between neighbours, all as she'd remembered it.

She switched off the TV and yawned. Last night she hadn't been able to sleep until four a.m. what with the clatter of bombs, fireworks and the explosion of petrol tanks in the distance.

By the time she'd walked to Sandy Row for her messages this morning, the only traces of the night's trouble were some telltale petrol slicks on the road, a molten shop sign, boarded shop windows and some ploughed-up earth in the pavement where saplings had been uprooted. But what was left was the buzz—no one could sweep that up, and the greengrocer had been quick to point the finger: 'Sure, it was all because the peelers bate the bollocks out of a couple of wee young fellas,' he had said, pursing his lips, swizzling the two corners of the paper bag round and round.

Things were even worse than in her day. If anything the Protestants here were now the new Catholics—hating everybody, fencing their small patch off from the chequerboard fields of the more vibrant Nationalist communities. They hadn't educated themselves. They'd thought that they'd be looked after forever but the big employers were all away now—Reid's, Gilpin's and, of course, the Belfast Brewery Co ...

'Take care,' had been her daughter's closing words on the phone. Formulaic words appropriate for a short journey to another town. She was glad that over in England her daughter would have no idea about the riots. She sank into wondering how her life would have been if she'd never been forced out of Belfast, if she'd never spoken to that boy. Paddy was his name. She hoped he'd made the most of his life, whatever that meant.

She walked up the stairs and watched the golden glow of the setting sun light up the shallow city basin within the hills, filling it like a shining dustbowl, silhouetting the far-off steeples of West Belfast. It was worth coming back for this view alone.

That day thirty years before in the brewery hadn't let go of her. It was she who'd tipped off Paddy, the Catholic worker, about the lynch mob that was coming to get him. It was her action that had led to the mob murdering a young Protestant boy by mistake.

Hoey and Merv walked through Boyne Court, past the cricket stumps painted on the wall, past the baskets of petunias hanging off the eaves, past the front rooms with their posies of flags in the vases instead of flowers. The streets were deserted as everyone was either in Sandy Row or at home. The last dapples of bright gold disappeared over the tops of the roofs. Dark clouds above the mountains were ruffled with virulent pink, like mould on the edges of a dying day, now past its best.

There was the sound of an explosion some streets away and Hoey grinned to himself.

They went up an alleyway blue with shadow. A boy of about eight was standing there, a crate double-tied around his waist with rope, and he was drumming slowly with two sticks painted red, white and blue. His cheeks were sunburnt, as pink as the clouds.

'Scoot!' ordered Merv, his eyes narrowing.

The boy slipped past them and then beat frenetically on the crate.

'Little scrote,' said Hoey, turning and making a few stamping steps in a mock run, at which the boy skedaddled.

Merv stopped outside one of the wooden gates.

'Way on! It's next door, you gimp,' whispered Hoey, shoving him on up the alleyway.

Hoey was breathing heavily as he pulled on the white surgical gloves. He put his hands to the top of the fence and hoisted himself over into the back yard, his boots slithering on the wood. Merv followed.

Pat heard the explosion and went through to the back bedroom. Black smoke was pouring into the sky. The helicopter swerved from its depths like a smoked-out wasp. There was an excited hysteria in her heart as there always was when she viewed something apocalyptic.

Just then, she noticed them down in the shadowy yard. The fading light caught the wet glints off one youth's hair, his grey sweatshirt appearing almost white. She didn't know whether to duck behind the curtain but instead, stood her ground and watched him stretch out a chalk-white hand. She could hear the faintest grind of the kitchen-door handle being tried. Then, a face swivelled up to her and she caught two eyes between a broad pug nose and the pitted skin through which the last of daylight ran.

'Locked,' whispered Hoey, allowing the door handle to slide upwards.

Merv took a backward step and looked up.

'She's there,' he said matter-of-factly.

Hoey swore and made to leave but Merv blocked the way.

'Do it!' Merv commanded. He didn't care now that the elderly lady with the face like his granny had seen him. He had right on his side.

Hoey took the stone out of his pocket and launched it at the glass of the back door. The glass shattered and Merv lit the rag at the top of the bottle and threw it, already turning and running, almost propelled by the smash and roar behind him.

They vaulted the gate and ran down the alleyway, their trainers making the pounding echo of footballs on concrete. As they entered the street, they slowed down and ripped off the gloves, stuffing them into their pockets. The pair walked sedately down Boyne Court as if out for a Sunday stroll.

'She'll tout on us,' said Hoey.

'An old doll like that can't see,' replied Merv briskly. 'Okay, we done it, so quit your crying.'

It was darker now. The mountains around Belfast were as black as coal lumps under the blue sky.

Hoey rubbed vigorously at the bandage on his arm, feeling it itch. Christ, he was going to going to make it bleed again. It had better look okay, the pitbull. He suddenly visualised himself with a sleeveless T-shirt revealing the bad-ass tattoo on his muscled arm while he sauntered along beside hardmen like Spence and McKee.

A youth with the hood of his sweatshirt up and a scarf wrapped round his lower face came hurrying from the direction of Sandy Row. Without mentioning it to each other, Hoey and Merv reflected that they'd have done the job better hooded up.

At Sandy Row, they finally saw the source of the black smoke. A burning bus barricaded the street and two blackened cars smouldered in front of it. The police landrovers were sitting at the top of Sandy Row, their lights trained.

Not far from the Royal where a crowd was gathered on Donegall Road, sat the Army Saxons.

'Why don't you go up the Falls?' a man was shouting bitterly at the Army. 'Call yourself Brits? You fucking sold us down the river!'

No one took any notice of the two youths, least of all the tall Canadian with the camcorder. His friends felt uncomfortable and decided to go back to the hostel but they left him their camera.

'I'll get you some good shots,' he promised them, slinging the camera across his shoulders like an ammo belt.

Pat scurried this way and that, trying to think of what to rescue, remembering she'd sold the garden hose. Finally she rushed outside, slamming the front door behind her and bent over double, coughing. When she looked up again, she could see flames flickering behind the glass inserts in the door.

'Dial 999, dial 999!' shrieked some women looking down from their bedroom windows.

There was a clack of army boots from a nearby alley and Pat's neighbour went to enlist their help.

She came back a minute later.

'It's mustard, Pat,' she said, shaking her head. 'The wee fucker with the fire extinguisher ran on without listening to a word.'

Pat jumped and cowered, as something crackled against the wall beside her.

'They're firing plastic bullets,' said the neighbour, aghast, pulling her aside.

Pat watched the hot smoke seep from the mouth of the letter box. An uncomprehending anger seized hold of her. She'd been on the blower to Peter Rea the day after her brother had died and he'd negotiated on her behalf. They'd told him it was all forgotten in these days of amnesty, that she was safe to visit, that the long exile was rescinded. She reflected that those boys couldn't have been much younger than the fella who'd been killed thirty years before.

About fifty rioters had convened at the edge of the housing on the Donegall Road. Hoey and Merv stood in the midst of them. The festive colours of the bunting rippled under bright streetlights. Hoey was eyeing up a couple of girls who were hanging around the fringes of the group, sitting on a wall. He'd seen them both before and he fancied the leggy, dark-haired girl in the jeans.

'See what we should do, we should get everywhere in Belfast to go off at the same time,' Merv was explaining to a small audience of lads. Out of the corner of his eye he noticed Hoey staring at the girls and his mouth grew even tighter with hatred.

Hoey couldn't hear what she was saying but he liked her quickfire tone and the hoarseness in her voice. She would definitely be up for a laugh.

Jackie Wright tugged at the scarf round his neck as if it were suffocating him and nodded towards the Canadian who'd stopped rolling his camera and was chatting to the bystanders up the road.

'That bastard got me on film. He might be a peeler-man,' he said quietly. 'What do you think?'

Merv watched Hoey walk towards the girls and replied, 'Aye, he mebbie is.'

The girls' names were Chelsea and Emma and they lived in Boyne Court but the riots had put them off going home.

'I'll escort you both,' offered Hoey and the girls laughed.

'Are you one of the untouchables, then?' teased the dark-haired girl who was called Chelsea.

'Depends who's doing the touching.'

Emma widened her eyes at his arrogance and gave an undulating mocking 'ooh'.

'So, you're taking me home tonight, then?' asked Chelsea, her eyes glittering.

'Oh, don't sound so desperate,' said Emma.

'Desperate? Thanks a lot,' replied Hoey, pretending to be hurt. He took out his smokes and offered them around.

'We don't want to go home yet, anyway. We might miss something,' said Chelsea.

He could tell she liked him the way she kept tilting her face towards him, then away.

Emma pointed out a new gush of smoke swirling into the sky.

'Jesus, would you look at that!'

'It better not be Boyne Court,' said Chelsea.

'I promise you it's not,' winked Hoey.

'And you would know, would you?' That came from Emma and Hoey decided she was jealous. He didn't like to be questioned. There was nothing worse than a doubt-caster. He frigging despised doubt-casters.

Merv saw the smoke too. He heard the fire engines in the distance but knew that they wouldn't risk driving into the estate till the riot was dispersed. He pictured the old woman again standing at the window with her baggy eyes and monkeyish lower jaw. As soon as their eyes had met, he'd sensed a calmness in her, a blank refusal to be intimidated. At that moment he had hardly been able to control his bowels. It had taken him several seconds to affect calm in return.

Girls' laughter rose above the hum of male voices. Merv went over to join Hoey with that familiar feeling of belonging mixed with fear of rejection. That blond chubby one was all right. Hoey had taken a lump of concrete embedded with shingle out of his pocket and was showing it to the dark-haired girl.

'See? It's like dinosaur skin,' Hoey was telling her and she was stroking the stupid stone. It was a lump of concrete for frig sake but Hoey had the girl eating out of his hand as always.

'All right?' Merv said to the chubby girl, noticing her eyebrows were the same colour as her hair.

'All right,' she replied, smiling.

The dark-haired girl nudged him. 'I think your friend's taking a hand out of me.'

'He's a top man. He'd do nothing for you,' he joked, relaxing.

Jackie Wright ran along the fronts of houses with a petrol bomb in his hand. A couple of plastic bullets clipped hollowly off the walls and Jackie froze like a scared spider, then dashed on again, unleashing the petrol bomb at a Saxon. It exploded and lit up the Saxon's underbelly and everyone cheered. Then Jackie dived behind a porch that jutted out like a sentry box.

'Go on! go on!' urged the girls, biting their lips and, when Jackie disappeared into the porch, they clenched their fists in the air and Chelsea flung her arm round Hoey. He'd felt the brief touch of her breast on his chest. With girls like that supporting you, you could do anything, thought Hoey.

He asked her if she liked clubbing. He'd have to get enough dabs to take her; he and Merv could steal another taxi driver's float like they did the week before. Mind, the taxi driver had chased them down the street with a steel chain, but he was too fat, he hadn't a mission of catching them. Sixty quid each in their sky rockets, they'd got. He'd spent it on the tattoo and Merv had spent his on his hair. He rubbed the white patch on his arm. He was sure it was infected. He imagined his arm going all green and reeking. Gangrene would set in. They'd have to amputate. Spence and McKee and that lot would call him the One-armed Bandit, he laughed softly while shivering. No, it didn't bear thinking about.

He wondered if Chelsea would sleep with him. He'd sneaked girls back to his mother's house before but tonight she wouldn't be asleep what with the riot raging on. Unless Chelsea had somewhere to go ... He eyed Merv and Emma. That girl, Emma, was a wee smart-mouth. He wasn't sure he liked her but at the same time he could hardly keep his eyes off her. Those rumpled lips under the lipgloss. As long as Merv didn't get any action either, he didn't mind.

Merv shifted uneasily as he weighed up what to say to Emma.

'If all parts of Belfast kicked off at the same time, the peelers would never cover it,' he began.

'He's a right serious-head, this one,' Emma said, nudging Hoey, who agreed.

'You haven't a bramble, have you?' Merv muttered.

He was disappointed. No girl ever cared what was happening to this city.

She gave him a sudden grin, though, that he softened to. The whole street was bathed in a carnival atmosphere. Some of the lads were throwing fireworks now and the colours were cracking and cartwheeling down the road. She had painted nails, he noticed, like tortoiseshell. It struck him as exotic.

The girls were twenty one, according to Chelsea but Hoey didn't believe a word of it. They looked like schoolies.

'How old are yous?' asked Chelsea.

'Twenty-four,' lied Hoey. He and Merv were both nineteen.

'You are not! Have I just come down the Lagan floating on a bubble?'

'Does it make a difference?'

'No, men's brains don't develop till they're twenty-five,' put in Emma, caustically.

'Aye, but he's hung like a donkey,' said Merv.

'Is that a big donkey or a little donkey?'

They all laughed but Hoey's laughter was tempered by his efforts to think of something smart to say in return. That Emma; he was vaguely disturbed by her, not fully realising that while she appealed to his egotistic sense of masochism, she ruffled his feelings of inferiority.

'Scatter!' shouted someone and they looked up the road to see a fleet of police landrovers careering towards them. Everyone started sprinting into the estate. Hoey put his hand out, searching for Chelsea, but she wasn't behind him. She and Emma had stayed where they were and were talking to two older men, two right hard nuts. He swore to himself and ran on. Girls were safe from the peelers, as were the older men.

The police in riot gear were pouring into the streets on foot. Already, most of the youths had dived into houses. Instinctively, Hoey and Merv ran down an alley that led back into Sandy Row. In front, they could see the misty charcoal skeleton of the hijacked bus and children picking through the rubble for the cases of plastic bullets.

They stopped and let their breathing rev down.

'We lost the girls,' said Merv ruefully.

Without the girls' company there was nothing to distract them from the memory of the old woman. They'd mucked it up big-style; the chances were she'd be able to identify them. McKee had said she was to be let alone. In the shop window next to Buzzin Badger's, there was a brief notice that stated: 'Anyone involved in anti-social activity will be dealt with.'

Hoey's mouth had gone dry. It had been Merv's idea. Merv said that it was, what were the words he'd used, indefensible for any community to keep traitors. Merv was talking too much bull now. He should never have listened to him.

He tried to remember the way Chelsea had looked at him, tried to recapture the tilt of her face as he stared through the heavy, burnt air. Children were still streetcombing and showing handfuls of what looked like black, shiny mussels to a community activist who counted them. The Canadian was busy filming, telling the children to hold out their spoils of war. 'That's great,' he kept saying.

From the opposite side of the street Jackie Wright winked at him.

Merv recalled the one small freckle on the bow of Emma's lips, almost imagining the warmth of her in the mild summery night.

Jackie fiddled at the scarf round his neck.

'Come here, mate,' he said to the Canadian. 'Wait till you see this.'

Hoey and Merv crossed the street to the alleyway. The Canadian was on the ground, rolling around under Jackie's feet. Hoey laid into him, uncertain of how much damage his trainers could do. Merv saw to the camcorder. Words he was learning to bandy around at The Ulster Society suddenly surged into his head in a harsh jumble with each separate kick, words that had recently become a conduit for his rage and hatred: condone, infringement, civil liberty, justifiable ...

Stalking Myths

'YOU'RE INSANE,' KIERON TOLD ANGELINA, AS they watched Bernard McLaverty leave in a taxi.

Angelina shrugged, sensing that the disapproval was scored with admiration. They'd been standing for fifteen minutes under the cherry tree outside the Queen's Common Room waiting for the man who looked like the novelist, Bernard McLaverty, to finish his pint and leave his friends. When he came out into the foyer, Angelina asked him if he really was Bernard McLaverty while Kieron stayed outside mortified under the blossom parasol of the tree.

'Are you a student of literature?' Bernard McLaverty responded and he seemed so certain she was; she nodded, accepting the only rational explanation.

'It probably looks like I'm stalking you but I promise you ... '

He smiled with his eyes as bright as polished buttons in a worn suit, said goodnight, then ran off for his taxi, moving crouch-legged under the rain like a spider.

'What did you want from him—his literary super-sperm?' said Kieron.

'You can be so bitchy.'

'I'm sorry. It's just you told me ... '

A few minutes later he was close to kissing her, so she ran away using the excuse that she was tired.

It was strange with the younger men. The more you told them you wanted to leave the singles world and settle down, the hotter they became. Like they'd just heard on the store intercom, 'Last minute sale in the Bargain Basement. Going Down!' At thirty-four, Angelina was ten years older than Kieron. He'd told her he'd been 'used for sex' by a thirty-six year old and the pristine vanity of this statement amused her.

She'd first met him at the Queen's Writers' Group. Some called it a writing group, but to her it wasn't so much about the writing as the writers. Joining the group in its post-discussion pub phase in the Queen's Common Room, she'd noticed him staring. Eye gridlock in Belfast was unusual because most men in pubs were too drunk to see beyond a five metre radius. And it was spring, a season which prompted her to say of him 'cute', a word that made her lips pucker into a kiss.

When he came to the Group after work, he was still in his suit and she loved how the arms of his shirt flared out from his slim-bodied waistcoat. The suit was pinstriped, the shirt checked and the tie spotted, a clash of patterns as if belonging to some composite exotic creature. And he was so dark, hairy with the black dog of Irish introspection crouched within him. She loved watching his innocent raised eyebrows as he spoke and the gradual wrinkling of his nose when he was about to say something nasty. She thought about him so much one night, the following day she went to the shop where she'd heard he worked. He was under the weather with a hangover and didn't express any real surprise in her tracking him down. That was how she knew he was for her. That and the massive North-Star pull to an earthy entanglement.

The next big night on Belfast's literary calendar was the Cathedral Quarter Arts Festival. One of the writers, Gavin, was going to interview the novelist Zadie Smith and was studiously quizzing the Group about possible questions. Angelina suggested asking why she had repackaged her name from Sadie Smith to Zadie Smith rather than

Sadie Zmith as that would have made her practically unique on the bookshelves with only some obscure foreign writers to jostle alongside her for book space. Gavin didn't think it was a burning question.

On Saturday she phoned up Kieron:

'Do you want to go to the Zadie Smith reading?'

'You aren't just phoning me because I asked you to ... '

'No, there is an element of want in it as well as duty, of course.'

'Want. You sounded almost passionate there.'

He was late when they met outside the Lagan Lookout but his appearance detracted from that. His hair was verging on the brilliantly audacious and absolutely dire. His sister had shaved his hair short and left a Mohican stripe down the centre, which was very brave considering the front of his hair was thinning. Like a last hair hurrah, thought Angelina.

He was a bit of a miracle worker on the fashion front, resurrecting the secondhand. He was wearing a 1960s tweed jacket with thin lapels and a new T-shirt with 'CAJUN' written across it.

'You haven't had the occ-Cajun to wear it until now,' she said but there was no reaction. 'My God, you're not quick to catch on, are you?'

A photographer from the *Ulster Tatler* snapped them both with the view of the Lagan in the background. Kieron wished afterwards he'd given someone else's name to the photographer for a joke.

'Who like? Bernard McLaverty?' she asked innocently.

'You stalker.'

'I wasn't stalking. I was networking.'

Kieron went to chat with a few others from the Group and Angelina overheard words like 'stalking' and 'Bernard McLaverty'. She noticed there wasn't any free wine about—it was clear that since she'd started going to literary events, the organisers had begun to reserve opening the wine until the interval—or perhaps that was just coincidence.

Zadie Smith came on to rapturous applause, blue jeans instead of blue stockings, in a sexy halter-neck top. She was lively but her eyes were sad.

She read a chapter from her follow-up novel to *White Teeth*. It was very erudite and paparazzi-ish at the same time. About Queen Victoria and Big Daddy, following their moves, observing them in the flesh, seemingly up close but from a distance, circling with her pen-cam, revering them, bringing them down to earth. Angelina could see at the side of the podium how scuffed Zadie's shoes were, worn down with walking, proof that she didn't just pound the pages. She remembered what the pastor had said about Pascale, the atheist, who, it was discovered on the day of his death, had 'Jesus is the way, the truth and the life' sewn into the seam of his jacket. She wondered what Zadie had sewn into the seams of her clothes. She glanced at Kieron, who was absorbed, and lost herself in the swirl of his stubble, black as lead filings, as wavy as a Van Gogh brushstroke. Like her mother said: spring flowers don't last.

'I've never read to such a quiet audience,' said Zadie, fazed, when the applause had quickly died. 'I'm not sure what to think.'

The audience asked her questions and Angelina put her hand up.

'Have you ever had stalkers?' asked Angelina, noticing that her voice seemed to come from somewhere in the rows in front of her.

Everyone laughed. The question wasn't for Zadie, it was for Kieron, but she didn't dare look sideways at him.

'Well, no, though I have had some very strange letters from a male prison in America ... '

After the last question was fielded, Zadie was ushered to the table of books for the book signing.

'Shall I invite her to the pub before the sycophants whisk her off?' Angelina asked the other writers but nobody seemed keen. Only when the event organisers gathered Zadie into their group, an American girl said regretfully, 'You should have asked her to come with us. That would have been really cool.'

Angelina felt like laughing. As if Zadie Smith could have jilted the sticky adulation of a literary rubdown to go out with them.

'Did you notice when she read,' said Kieron, 'how she wipes her nose a lot? She copied that from the Martin Amis cocaine-snorting nose-wipe.'

The Americans headed off to see the Billy Bragg concert but Kieron and Angelina decided to go on their own to Bittle's Bar. The streets as usual in the city centre were dead except for the occasional door opening that piped out music and people who then vanished into taxis.

Glancing over her shoulder, Angelina saw that Zadie Smith's group was about twenty metres behind them.

'Zadie Smith's stalking us.'

Kieron witnessed the Zadie Smith group turn into one of the chrome and glass bars that had grown up all over Belfast. Fish bowls with black piranhas guarding them.

'Stalking usually involves following,' he explained sarcastically.

When Angelina was small, she believed that her mum had the supreme power to prevent bad things happening to her. She kept this ultimate faith until she was ten when she realised her mother's reassurances that she wouldn't have to wear glasses for long were ridiculously hopeful. Even to this day she could still see her mum standing at the door of her bedroom, insisting, 'I'm telling you. I say so and that's that!' She already knew that she began with faith in her mother and would end her life with faith in God, that she needed this faith, that she needed to be constantly watched. Which went hand in hand with constantly watching.

Bittle's Bar had paintings of Irish writers on its walls stretching from the floorboards to the rafters. There was the famous photograph of Samuel Beckett resembling a leathery-skinned Indian called Hawk Nose. At the back of the pub was a giant painting of the Irish greats all standing drinking at a bar: Yeats, Behan, Friel, and what looked like Joyce only one of the spotlights was trained too harshly on his face.

'They must be blotting out James Joyce's face on purpose,' said Kieron with the air of the cognoscenti.

'Why's that? For being an obscure prat?'

'No, because he was too great.'

Angelina's eye was drawn towards Brendan Behan's shock of black hair which shot up like a vertical Afro.

'You can idolise Joyce, but you're in the direct literary hairline of Behan,' she pointed out.

You didn't notice it on first glance at the scene, but the bartender was Oscar Wilde looking laconic with a treble cherry brandy in his glass. He was clearly bored with the company, probably like poor Zadie Smith would be feeling right now.

'Had a bit of a stint the other night,' was the chat round the bar.

A vinous-looking man who ran a hairdresser's started chatting to them.

'I've seen worse,' he said of Kieron's mohican and Kieron rolled his eyes and stuck his tongue out through his teeth shyly at Angelina, who laughed. 'Sure, his hair is fucked anyway. He's losing it like me. You need your hair styled,' he informed Angelina. 'How many years have you had it like that?'

'One,' said Angelina, wondering if it was like that since she was born.

'No, more,' insisted the incisive and cutting hairdresser.

'Well, I had it longer.'

'Longer but the same.'

'You can style it for her,' suggested Kieron.

'If I wanted to deal with mops, I'd have been a cleaner,' he said, swinging back round to his own group.

'You know,' said Kieron, 'This is the first time we've been out together and he's just torn our heads off in front of each other.'

'Better without illusions. Did you see Zadie Smith's bum-cleft out of her low-cut jeans during the book signing?'

Her own arse had been much accoladed in the nineties. She'd won 'Rear of the Year' in a pub in Kent, though it had undergone a few fluctuations since then.

She couldn't help thinking of the thousands of people she had passed by and passed over in all those years. The thing was, they were still with her. She could picture them in the time and place she'd met them and know they'd moved on, but they'd be in a similar sort of place years on. There were no fish out of water. Fish out of water cannot breathe. So she could see them exactly, aged and in their natural environment.

She looked at his forearms. The black hair on the creamy skin reminded her of Guinness.

Younger, gaudier customers started filtering in and the older men, who'd been looking at their pints like they were hourglasses, started to say their goodnights. Angelina shivered at the cold air from the open door and Kieron got up and closed it for her.

The landlord rushed to the door in a rage.

'What are you playing at?'

'My friend found it cold.'

'Cold?' bristled the landlord, arching his back. You could make his belly button out through the T-shirt distended thinly over his fat belly. 'Are you away in the head or something?'

He stomped back to the bar, chin furled into his neck like a speculative cobra. Kieron sat back down, dismayed.

'You got shouted at because you were being nice to me. It wasn't fair,' Angelina consoled him.

Suddenly the lights went out and a big disco ball on the ceiling started spraying coloured light. Seamus Heaney didn't look too happy about it. He didn't seem comfortable anyway in his portrait with his two heads, one greenly sprouting out of his neck like a nobuled growth on a spud, or enjoying its first stage of turning into a bog body.

They started on the long walk to her house. The city felt like a damp cellar with trickling walls beneath the hills.

'You're cold. Do you want to take my coat?' he asked.

'No, but I'd take the trousers off you.'

They joined hands.

'This is what Shakespeare called paddling,' said Kieron, sliding his hand against hers.

'If that's paddling, I want to go swimming.'

Flirting, flirting all the way.

Being back in her own house made her sober. She poured them some beer and they sat down together.

'I like the way you touched me just then,' said Kieron.

'What way?'

He showed her how she'd put her hand round his inner thigh and squeezed it just as they'd sat down. She'd no consciousness of doing it.

'But we can never be together long term,' she explained and a feeling came over her like the pain and whiteness before the blood rises to the surface, mingled with all those stifling conflictions—I don't want to have to phone him, yet I don't want to wait for his call; I don't want to go and live with him yet I don't want him to move in with me ...

It was a feeling like being hidden behind the long branches of a weeping willow.

He noticed that her attic bedroom was very dark, even under bright electric light. He noticed that the walls were yellow, the madness colour. They made unsatisfying love to each other as though the magnetism was actually driving them apart, transforming into allergy. He revealed afterwards he was on Seroxat for depression which explained his inability to come. Angelina couldn't help thinking of semtex.

'That's why we're so connected: I'm manic and you're depressive, you're introspective and I'm extrospective, you're a soul-stalker, I'm a people-stalker.'

'But why don't you kiss me?' he wanted to know.

In the morning Kieron watched her stir.

'Let me see your morning face, Angelina.'

'What if I was an old wrinkled crone lying here?'

'What do you mean, "What if?"'

Kieron imagined how Zadie Smith might write about sex in her new novel.

'It was a night of one body clenched to another as a spider crouches to the ceiling or stuff like that, of that kind of nature,' he read aloud from his imagination.

'Or in *White Teeth* it would be, "Do you want eggs and chips or eggs and sex and chips?"'

'"Do you want eggs and chips and spam or eggs and chips and a shag?"'

'"Do you wants eggs and chips or legs and tits?"'

They went on, doubled up with laughter.

In a hotel room Zadie Smith shifted, sleeping lightly, encumbered by some far-off dream of words, her subconscious disturbed that the Belfast audience had been so quiet and watchful.

'Will we see each other again outside the Group?' asked Kieron.

'Perhaps.'

'I don't think we will,' he sighed.

'No, but I will see you.'

She remembered the day she stopped and looked at the Bobby Sands mural on the Falls. 'Hello, Bobby,' a woman had greeted him on her way shopping. And the time she met a community worker in the Shankill who said they really wanted tourists to come to the area. 'See that mural of the sniper?' he said enthusiastically: 'Isn't it style? The barrel of his gun follows you wherever you go.' Watched and followed. Stalking the lives of saints and heroes. It wasn't weird in the Ulster psyche.

When the next edition of the *Ulster Tatler* was out, it had the photo of Kieron and Angelina standing together. Angelina was so surprised, her hand touched the page to make sure. There, behind Angelina's left shoulder, stood Zadie Smith, looking bemused.

Undergrowth

WARSAW'S SHADE THIS MORNING IS A monotone grey. The Daewoo building is a hard matrix of grey and black stripes against the formless misty sky. A bus passes, full of workers wearing multifarious colours, the forward-facing robots who can't dream. Their facial topology is a desert. They've forgotten about the undergrowth, waking each morning with a deeper nescience than the day before. They've retreated to their own world at the back of their brains, let their senses fall into disuse and it's almost too late for them to see the undergrowth of tangled life which surrounds them and, if they did, their urge might be to destroy it.

8.00 a.m. A woman is sitting on the bus, her sandalled feet tucked under her seat, hidden from marauding strangers. She's eating cherries from a bag. Her swift, hungry movements transform her into a forest animal devouring the fruits of a tree. A squirrel perhaps or a mongoose with magnified eyes behind glasses but, whatever species, she's a shy animal with a bob which swings forward and conceals her mouth. Not a bobtail but a bobhair.

She feeds herself with one of her large, muscular, ultradextrous paws, then strips the stone of its meat with her prominent front teeth, no more than a moment's work, and promptly ejects the stone into the palm of her other hand. Now and then you catch a flash of nails shining like lacquered wood.

She eats the fruit as if it's a rare treat, a berry feast on which she must binge to fortify herself for the winter of work. One can only guess that as soon as she gets to the office, she will hibernate under her desk. A stone slips out of her cupped hand and she's momentarily concerned because she's a clean, tidy creature but it's nowhere to be found in the folds of her clothes, so she carries on feeding.

The strips and bands of buildings grow with confidence in the foreground. Like giant redwoods, they begin to blot out the sky and the clearing of road that the bus follows faintly darkens.

There is a rustle as the woman ties the bag of cherries. She gets up to go and she's left behind a couple of stones in the seat corner, like little droppings.

8.30 a.m. A denim-clad boy of nineteen or twenty has boarded the bus. He's blond unlike most of the people who sleep in the street but he has the same street-scars—a street-scar named desire: the zigzag scar down the nose and the fresh grazes like red stubble on the mouth and neck, caused from a viral skin disorder or falling over in a drunken fight.

A blond gypsy-heart, a fallen angel with his robes caught in the gutter, he's most likely a Russian émigré fleeing from the Mafia mark of death. He can save money from his labouring work by sleeping rough in summer but, even so, he sleeps in the workers' hostel one night a week to get cleaned up, so he doesn't turn completely feral.

He stands at the back of the bus holding a dozen plants, freshly ripped from the earth, taken from someone's private property. You can see the white bones of their roots to which the soil is clinging tangentially. With every brake and acceleration, the boy jerks back and forth like a puppet on a string worked by the driver's feet and the soil flies onto the shoulders of people in the aisle seats.

When the hail of soil hits them they look up in a temper but a second later they quail.

Because, look, the boy has the stare of someone who has no pride, no shame, no shyness, no ego, no particle of human construct whatsoever. And yet why does it seem he asks sophisticated questions to which there are no answers? It is the simple stare of an animal at the top of the tree, of curiosity without hostility. He is quite content with his individual transaction with fate and he's observing no more than a bunch of curios. Everyone shifts uncomfortably because he can see through the flimsy businesswear that protects them like the design on an empty vase. They are disembodied and he penetrates right through to their empty inner world, which is also enlivened by a few bright designs. Unknowingly, he obliterates them.

There are homemade tattoos in the outer corners of the boy's eyes—just a little tick of blue and one larger blue dot on the eyelid. He's the avatar of an ancient blond tribe. The tattoos empower his eyes which are weak and watery blue. He runs his tongue over his soured lips, tinctured with deep red. He's just had his own liquefied fruit breakfast of cranberry vodka and there's a pain growing in his stomach. He blinks. He can sense a spark in the air, a presentiment of inchoate life that makes him happy. He knows no word for it but it is the undergrowth quietly at work.

He reaches his stop and a pale sun emerges, a light shining through the papery sky.

9.00 a.m. A man hauls a striped bag on wheels onto the bus and sits down heavily. He's wearing a fedora which he lifts momentarily to wipe away the sweat, revealing greased-down hair like a seal puppy's head. His hair is mainly black but beneath it is a face that has been folded, concertina-ed, fanned out, crushed and crumpled into a ball of emotion and finally opened.

He sniffs at the morning air loudly, trying to find the earth's rhythm. He's not fully awake and gives a yawn, biting on his knuckle. The yawn soars above the bus's drone. It's like he's high-amped, functioning on a more voluble frequency than the people around him.

He watches a girl who's feverishly engrossed in dreams, her head blown about on its stem by swaying images. Some waking force inside him coltishly desires to break through the doors to her consciousness.

The bus is full of cataleptic semi-sleepers, their eyes blindly turned inward, shifting with thoughts of the day's work. The man realises with surprise that what he took to be the insect hum of the engine is in fact the low brain-buzz of interior monologues around him.

He scratches his neck and shoulder and his fingers crackle against the material of his old stone-coloured suit. His skin has the pungency and desiccated consistency of old banknotes. His face is full of strata, deep-fissured from life's hard knocks. Perhaps he was born in some distant geological age. His scars are like old embedded fossils—a white shoal of petrified fish is swimming across his neck.

He lifts a bottle of beer from his bag and cracks it open with a bottle opener extracted from his inside pocket. With closed eyes he raises his lips to the bottle neck like dry petals unfurling to the rain. He drinks and his cheeks move in and out with the relish of pumping biceps. He lowers the bottle and his breath explodes in a long, satisfied 'Aah … ' He tries to wink at someone but their glance, like a frightened moth, has flittered away and merged into the dull distance.

He brings something out of his pocket and puts it on. It's a party set of glasses, red nose and moustache.

'Good, this beer,' he says, in case no one has noticed his comical transformation, his audacious pleomorphic illusion. It would be hard not to. A couple of smiles steal out from the enclosed boxes of faces. All too few.

He drops the bottle. It hits the floor with a thud and spins round, pumping out beer. He swears and bends down to get it but his hat falls off and he swears again. The glasses frame is in the line of his vision. His fingers are covered in a messy concoction of soil and beer and he rubs them on his trouser leg. He tries to drink what's left but he has difficulty getting the bottle neck past his low-slung plastic moustache.

An elderly woman's sitting a few seats up wearing a pink beret which looks like a breast with a nipple. It really does. Restrained laughter wrinkles his face. He meets the gaze of a woman opposite him. She has slanty green eyes like a cat and a face pasty with anger and there are tiny veins on her cheeks like angry red hieroglyphs written from within.

So many people wrapped up in their morning cocoons and he can't reach out to them. He's done his best to communicate but he's trapped on his own isthmus, standing on a lonely promontory, separated by a closed border of minds from the vast land mass.

At the next stop he gets off.

Sunshine is beginning to swarm into every cool corner. The bus stops at the lights and in the driver's mirror there's a shuttle of heads. Pages in someone's book shatter and skip, a woman's flowers splatter colour everywhere, faces splinter then fuse and the light on the window's rubber edge expands into a blinding atomic light filling the whole space.

10.00 a.m. was the agreed hour for the drivers' strike. The buses left their appointed routes and went back to the depot. Unexpectedly, by noon the government hadn't caved. By noon the next day they hadn't caved either and there were reports that they were considering drafting in the army as replacement drivers. It took four days before negotiations resolved the strike.

The big news was the end of the strike. But as usual the real miracle didn't even make it into the day's footnotes.

In the morning the doors to the depot were raised. Light scattered like a seed-head, blowing away the inner shadows but the buses resolutely blocked out the rays, each short black tunnel of steel, swollen with darkness, exuding a strangely charged somnolence.

A driver went to her bus and opened the doors. The damp mustiness flooded out as it did on many mornings after rain but on this occasion there was something unusual, a light essence in the dank brew, a young distending sweetness triggering the smallest recollection of a spring scent. The fragrance confused her. She ascended the steps into the dark corridor and thought she could hear a noise like a gentle foaming or a low rustling from somewhere inside.

She walked slowly up the bus and her eyes widened as she knelt down.

It was growing riotously between the seats out of the fermented humus. From its tangle of slender branches, green shoots pushed out to greet her. It was a wondrous sight. From the mixed-up chaos of human energy, a small cherry tree had been born.

Postcard from Heaven

MY PIANO TEACHER SAID, 'I BELIEVE in geniuses,' as someone might controversially declare a belief in ghosts or fairies. She believed that I was a genius but she was angry I didn't practice all the hours God sent. I wondered where God sent all these hours from—were they on loan from Heaven?

At home my mother was fed up with my late nights out. She said, 'Paganini was locked in an attic till he played perfectly.'

I chipped in, 'I heard that Colette's husband locked her in the apartment to make her write.'

Without really thinking, my own words sealed my fate. I was to stay in all summer to perfect my God-given talent, a summer of inspiration insulation against the outside world.

That was hard but I looked in the mirror and told myself I could face it.

I live on the tenth floor with an outlook onto flat concrete tops and baggy roofs embedded with sleepy hooded windows. On the edge of the city the mist is like the smoke of a burning autumn, inflicting its golden-patched disease on us.

I play a few minutes of Chopin to an angry wasp headbanging in the corner of the window. Then I look down and my hand tendons lead down to my knuckles like a clam, the fingers completely retracted into my palm. There's nothing to be done.

The roofs are the juice of preserved plums, compote cherries in these apple-wine days. A man is mending a roof, sitting on its seam-stitched ridge like a jockey, and I roar him on to go faster and faster to outstrip the other roofs. Leaning forward, he bangs his hammer down and the thuds rack through the sky.

Below, in the street, a young man about to be ordained, carrying a priest's outfit, is sprinting to church.

I open the window and cheer him on.

'God waits for no man!' I yell.

Being inside makes me cruel. On the balconies opposite, pale duvets and pillows are yellow and plumping in the sun, big pears soaking in the watery juice of day and I want to bite into them.

In the distance my mother, flossy-haired in the light like a dandelion seed head, her figure a silvery grey of dried-out weeds, is walking towards our block. She looks up at me, maybe even hopefully but I can't give her that.

I close my window carefully. One day under a muffled sky of suffocating pillows, I was practising and the cloud in great calcified lumps sailed in and pushed me to the walls, so naturally I never play now with the window open.

My parents couldn't expect me to play constantly. So sometimes I sat and contemplated whether coffee and cigarettes or beer and cigarettes were more divine. Or I chatted to the pigeon walking along the pavement of my window sill. I tasted the wall—an imaginative combination of cold chalk and lemons—and put the insects' buzz-balm on my eyes. And how pretty was the lit bare wall behind the moving lace curtain in whose shivering net reflection white butterflies were caught. What could I create without music? Only tears, and I tried to form a vale of tears but I realised it was impossible to compose more than a lake or a river. And I experienced a great chopping and heightening of mood.

I don't want to give the impression that my room, cream-painted and wood-panelled was or is a bleak trap. It's filled with coloured scarves, painted bark, laughing photos and candles and soft lamps. Sometimes the room will still rebel against my utter domination. A card or photo like a leaf twists on its stem and crackles against the wall, floating to the floor like burnt ash. And the debris on the floor will out-crackle the mummified leaves, resembling a pulped carpet walking into winter.

I've noticed all sorts of things—that the crow eats with its head upside down and music is a food-drug to keep thoughts cheery, but the day when something awful happens ... What happens then? Can you stand your inner silence?

I eat the pastry that's been sitting here since lunch. The bread tastes of fermented wine, damp and vinous. It's a warm, autumn day and I feel hot like a dog left in the back seat of a sunny car. Thankfully, dusk will soon come, an amalgam of grey filling the bright raw nerve of the day. My father's come home and I can hear them in the living room, the news switched on like it's of national importance to them. When they talk about young people deserting morality and the church, black puddles of dusk grow in their eyes, spreading, dampening the light. I watch a flock of birds escaping and the setting sun flattens out in the low cloud skewer like liquid filling a receptacle and you can look at it, anvilled between the clouds, captured. Then it's taken down beneath the buildings black as headstones in its cloud coffin emblazoned with holy light.

As I watch, I am standing with my hands on my hips, a posture I inherited from my grandmother. I know this, although I can't actually see myself in the mirror, because I've swathed a scarf over it. I haven't looked at myself in months, not since my reflection which was happy at first to be purely representative, decided to rebel and become symbolic. I wasn't angry. It would be oversensitive to take the mirror's reshaping of my image as personal rejection. I suppose with perpetually having me in the room, it was only natural that it would little by little take on its own appearance, bored by my predictability and informed by its background perceptions. On the wall the painting of the Virgin Mary looked shocked but there it was.

The delight of that first postcard from my friend on holiday in the mountains! Then the second and the third, postcards from Heaven! And I was lapping at the lakes of white shadows, at the pink shale sunsets and chalky mountain paths forking into an aching-blue blue and the bright green candles of spring forests. I could almost feel the 'halni,' the biting wind that sends the highlanders crazy. And that very night a gale howled in the kitchen vent and the outer door shuddered on its hinges and I opened my window and it snatched away my glove like a baleful sacrifice. The wind took away one hand that night, stole it from music's clutches.

But it's true you can't stay long on the tenth floor. The sky is so infinite, that space so inviting and like a bird you want to dive into it a thousand times. My parents saw this; they weren't tyrants. They wanted to take me to the forest but I told them I would practise instead. So, they brought me back a woody brown fungus like a giant ear that had listened to the secrets of the forest and would now, by the unwitting act of being plucked by my parents, be forced to listen to music.

It's night. I pour wax from the candles over my hand. It's painful at first, then the wax hardens coolly and encases my skin in a glove which I then crack by playing some notes. I turn out my light. My parents think it's all black in here when they look through the smoked-glass pane in my door, but in fact I'm in a little infra-orange world behind the black glass and I can see everything around me like it's lit up by burning filaments of copper wire curls. My mother's clinking in the kitchen pouring out another glass of 'herbal' tonic, full of natural goodness and nicotine and alcohol.

The hall light goes out and the glass in the door is total black. Now my room is lit up by infra-white light streaming through the window. The white crepe ball lampshade is a big moon growing in confidence as outside, the moon, prostrate with the cold, curls up. I can hear truncated, elongated cries, strange canorous whistles and doors slamming and I imagine if everyone in the world were to shut their doors at once. Maybe tonight I'll hear the tramp, inspired by the Philharmonia Concert Hall, spinning out on the spools of the wind her beautiful little reels of song and I wonder if she's heard of Paganini.

An hour later I went out. I escaped down the metal rubbish chute. Not that this means of exit aided my escape; it was simply more interesting than descending by lift. I went to a club I know where I got chatting to a man with a downy beard and eyes like jet-lagged diamonds. He had just broken up with his girlfriend because she'd slept with others, overused his credit card and wouldn't clean the house.

'When you are in love, the world is very small,' he told me. His forehead was cushioned with worry lines.

'The world is very small,' I agreed. What did I know?

He put a cigarette in his mouth and talked more, the words dancing and waggling down the white tightrope, but I couldn't understand and left him to dance and I danced like a demon until we were the dregs of the night, the last grains left in the bowl of the dance floor, flowering into disordered, segmented half-rainbows in the mirrors of electric eyes. I ran back home with crosswaves of whirls traversing my head, three thoughts forward, then one giant thought back and the thump of feet was beat music and the swish of a coat circumscribed a smile, my clothes torn on rose briars of darkness, and I couldn't tell what drugs I'd forged in my brain.

And I slipped right back into the pocket of wooden-lined stone. My mother heard me come in and her hope rose. Bottle clink-clink.

Good morning! I fling open the window and the cold cup of nature throws itself into my face. Leaves fly up vertically like birds, then swoop and plummet on the thermals, bombs on an arc, speeding on the grace of nature's admiration for invention and nerve. In the wind's whirlpool, feathers are sucked up, sycamore seeds, one-winged dragonflies, babies' crying ... The coral wall outside is bubbling plaster. I sit at the piano, for once longing to play, and the notes are shot through like leaves by the bullets of autumn and are dragged into the wind's spiral shutters and the old woman waves her arms like a conductor on the balcony and the deep cinnabar carpet swirls open and closed, envelops her like a ball gown.

It is over one year since my parents locked me in. Last September when I auditioned for the academy they said I wasn't going to cut it, I couldn't make the grade. My parents then begged me to go out and I told them I knew that good was a circle, evil was a square, but I still wouldn't leave the box as I was passionate to pursue the pianist's dream.

I yank the scarf off the mirror and it flies into the vortex. I let loose a flotilla of perfect notes, inverse swans' heads, and they soar and flock to the other cliff tops, entangling themselves in the washing lines, vibrating there, hanging within the gussets of underwear. People laugh rejoicingly, and, when I appear at the window they point at me and suddenly bow their heads in amazement.

'It's the 10, 153rd emanation of Our Lady on this Earth!' they exclaim.

What a superb trick! My appearance, weak from not having the verity of its own existence validated in the mirror, had abjectly decided to conform to its reflection, mischievously borrowed from the only other female manifestation in the room. The Virgin Mary in the picture looks startled at my apotheosis in her image and suddenly I'm so happy, my heart bursts out from the blasted circle of my chest.

My mother sobs quietly in the kitchen, pouring herself a glass of tonic.

The Experimental Girlfriend

SHE SAID SHE WAS FROM ST. Petersburg. Was she from the Ukraine? She wasn't educated. Of course she knew Dostoyevsky but she didn't know Solzhenitsyn.

Liam stared across at the square-holed dovecotes, the balconies of the apartments opposite. A hundred TVs were on, flickering like a lightning storm in the building, a code of successive dusks and lights and darks, a holy blue. He was thinking about the old man's story of the Russian soldiers coming to his home in 1945, how they were savages, stealing everything, shooting at the cuckoo clock. The Russians had had no fear because they'd been brainwashed into believing they were immortal and that not so much as a bullet could harm them.

Alex looked over and grinned suddenly.

Liam had met Alex three weeks after arriving in Poland when his Swedish friend, Tony, invited him to this 'club' out in the country. It was Tony who'd brought her for Liam for the night but even Tony —and Tony was mad; he was dating two mafia girls behind their boyfriends' backs—even he'd said not to do it, not to let her get so close but for Liam 'don't do it' was a red light that had to be jumped.

Alex had brought her things round the next day in a pitifully small suitcase.

Right now she was wearing his T-shirt and his socks, which made him laugh because the heel bagged out lumpily at her ankle. She was sitting on the bed with the nail file in her hand. Sometimes she'd dig it into her skin like a scalpel, peeling back the layers, tunicate as a Russian doll. At this rate she'd file her beauty down into a little pile of wood shavings. There was a black shine on her parted hair catching the light bluely, soaking it up into its dark quivering puddles, that rim of snow gleaming under her bark-brown eyes. She never wore make-up in the house. Her face was pale brown like dry earth or dead bronze corn.

'Baby,' she said and beckoned him over. She got him to touch a tumid lump on her leg and sucked in the air with pain. He rubbed it better. Two years ago she'd jumped out of an apartment window in the Ukraine and injured it.

She couldn't speak English but her Polish was perfect and Liam's friend, Wojtek, had translated some things for him. Liam knew only a little about her—that her father had beaten her and her mother had tried to sell her to the first man that came along. What had attracted him was her energy. 'My little Kalashnikov,' he called her. She mock-fought him a lot and gave him a fireman's lift home from the pub when he was drunk. 'Russki,' she'd say proudly, flexing her arm. 'She says she will kill you if you don't go running with her tomorrow morning,' Wojtek had translated. 'She can win in any race. Tomorrow, she will be running away from you.' 'Ah, but I'll be running away from her in six weeks when I go home to Ireland,' Liam had replied and she'd laughed but he'd felt guilty about that one.

He took another toke on the joint. Julian, who used Liam's flat as a post-pub drop-in, bolted a shot of vodka, dropped his jaw and screwed up his eyes, trying to hide his face in his shoulder which made Alex burst into laughter.

Alex's friend, Kristiane, laughed too. She was curled on the bed behind them browsing through a *Real* magazine, murmuring about the delicacies she'd like to eat.

In three weeks I'm skedaddling, he reminded himself. He'd set up the office and recruited a lot of Polish labourers. It was now up to his brother in Ireland to get the contractors; but the boys back home preferred cheapness over quality and were happy enough with the workers from Nigeria, Senegal ...

His mobile rang.

'Hi, it's Tony.'

'Tony! How's it going?'

'Not bad. Look, I found something out about Alex you're not going to like.'

'Oh?'

'Friend of Patricia's was supposed to fix up a flat for Alex in Warsaw but she didn't do it, so Alex sent round two men to smash things up.'

'No. It's not the sort of her to do that.' Alex was laughing again. She'd laughed at a slapstick film on TV once, at the really cruel parts.

'I'm telling you, man, be careful how you break up with her.'

Sure, he knew she had friends who could hurt him. First night she came, a man called round to check up on her, even though she'd said her boss was a very good woman who was content to let her go. She was still nervous whenever the doorbell rang. At that nightclub the Russian doorman who'd shaken hands with him was covered in blood. At the Russian market, Alex's friends looked at him with shaded eyes, evaluating him.

Sure, she wasn't like that; Julian for one thought she was fantastic.

Kristiane opened Liam's litre of whiskey. She was a hard dark shadow behind Alex. Alex's fringe was soft, hers was not, though she had the plucked eyebrows of a saint. Some psycho called her yet again on her mobile and Alex grabbed it and deep-breathed down it, then she, Kristiane and Julian fell about in stitches.

Strange. Alex had shaped curvy lips from the front view but from the side view nothing. No substance to her appearance. She had a broad Slavic face but starved strait-leathered legs. She'd made those leather trousers herself. Funny, but Liam always noticed that the people with the most vices had the greatest talents. Or perhaps their bad past just highlighted the skills they were capable of bringing to the world. No, she was a good girl.

A plate of cold red watermelon lay on the floor. She loved ice-cold fruit and the old Russian fridge in the kitchen froze the life out of everything.

Her grey-valleyed eyes were closing again. She was often sleepy these days, those long eyelashes like a broom sweeping away the truth.

Julian said he was going.

'I'll lend you money for a taxi.'

A hundred zloty were missing out of his wallet. It was the second time. He glanced at Alex. Her eyes were closed. He'd speak to her about it tomorrow. Only reason he'd let it go before was because she was kind. She gave leftover food to the tramp who slept by the bins—or had he let it go because he expected it, accepted it as his punishment?

A hand was creeping up his thigh. No, he said, pushing Kristiane away. She swore at him, then ran into the bathroom and he heard her puking. He knocked on the door to see if she was okay and she burst out, screaming and slapping, then rushed back in and slammed the door on him.

He slipped into bed beside Alex. She was fast asleep, grinding her teeth, and he rolled her onto her side to make her stop.

At about three a.m. she woke him up. She was moaning and gripping her stomach. She'd had on-off pains for days but this was serious. He drove her to the hospital and she was rushed into casualty. While he was waiting, he kept thinking of his favourite image of her standing at the door, long-legged, in nothing but his T-shirt and pulling him to bed and it made him pray for her. When he was allowed in, the doctor told him that her ovaries had swollen. She showed him an x-ray and all he could make out was a big black patch in a swirling white galaxy of miniature stars. He went for a walk outside and looked up at the stars. He cried a little. There was nothing new under the sun but in other galaxies there was plenty. He remembered phoning his older sister the day after Alex moved in.

'I'm with a Russian girl now. Well, I'll tell you the story when I get back. It's a hell of a story.'

'Liam. Not another new girl.'

'You know me. I want to see it all.'

'For goodness' sake. D'you know what you would say if you were on the way to Heaven? Would you just let me off at hell for a minute to have a gawk?'

Alex was kept in hospital for twenty-four hours. Initially, the nurse came to the flat to give Alex injections, then Alex did it herself. She stayed in bed all day while he went to the office. She painted her filed-down nails deep purple like the retracted buds of trees in winter and got him to dye her hair black. One night he was at his friend Karolina's when Alex phoned. She went crazy with jealousy, thinking the sound of the washing machine in the background was Liam and Karolina having sex. Liam laughed it off, putting it down to the heavy medication.

When she was feeling better, he took her for a walk. She was in the new clothes he'd encouraged her to wear—a tartan skirt and a jumper to her midriff and she was cold beneath her jacket and angry with him. It was a day when the sun's colours were being sucked out like a coloured ice cube by the fog's tongue. Black clouds passed over it highlighting its outline—a black resinous aureole. They walked along the path of the canal, its chunting dark blood in a white tube of snow. The path had been swept of snow as if gouged out by a finger leaving a furrow of white tissue on either side. But the day, though bleak, cheered her up and she laughed, playfully trying to get him to skinny dip with her.

'She's stealing from you,' said Wojtek when Liam complained about the amount of marijuana Wojtek gave him for a hundred zloty. 'She only gave me sixty zloty.'

He confronted her that night and she cried. He would have given her the money if she'd asked. After he stormed out, she phoned up promising to tell the truth about herself if he came home. She told him she used to smoke opium, she'd been to prison twice and she tried to explain something more but he couldn't understand and she lost her temper. She filed her nails and cut herself. She scared him. It was now a case of how to get rid of her without trouble. He could just leave her there and find himself another flat when he returned to Poland. He wouldn't find somewhere, though, with a better location. Maybe he could tell the landlord the situation and get him to pretend that they had to move out before Christmas.

The next night Liam couldn't have been more delighted when Alex mentioned she was thinking of taking a sewing job in a factory in another city. She went out to meet someone about it and was optimistic when she returned. It appeared that the situation was happily resolving itself.

She went out another time to see about the job. When he asked her how it went, she was non-committal. She slipped off her trousers and lay on the bed, tired again. He looked at her legs. She had a tattoo on her ankle of a rose surrounded by briars. The briars seemed to grow up her leg, to even peep out in the shadow of her neck. His hand holding the joint was shaking.

Her behaviour was changing. When he looked for a pen, she would shout 'No,' and rush to get him one herself. She insisted on drying him when he came out of the bath. One night he woke up alone and found her sitting in the kitchen reading a book with the gas rings on for warmth. She was sitting up to ensure he got a good night's sleep because she knew her grinding teeth disturbed him. Finally, he persuaded her to come back to bed.

The issue had to be ironed out.

'You know I have to go back to Ireland in a week, don't you?'

'Yes.'

She said matter-of-factly that she'd move out and spend Christmas with a friend but hoped he would contact her when he came back to Poland. He relaxed. It was that Tony's fault for making him paranoid. She was cool about it and now he didn't worry about himself, he worried for her.

She'd developed full-blown going-out-itis, complaining of pains in her eyes, sitting like a tired Madonna engrossed in a Mills-and-Boon type book. It unsettled him to watch her, her unsmiling down-tilted face in shadow except for her forehead touched by light. Reluctantly, she got dressed to go out one night.

It was a disaster. They went to a club where Liam met some friends and spent time talking to them. Alex hitched up her skirt and danced sexily with any man she could grab, then when she failed to raise Liam's jealousy, ran out. Liam could have let her go but he thought that he should go easy, play the game. There were only a few days left with her.

She was waiting round the corner. More falsely brewed tears!

She'd tell the truth if he came home. Well, he was sick of this silver little hook of truth but would hear her out anyway.

The truth was she was on heroin. She'd started at the time she'd met him.

The syringes from her illness were still at home, that lump on her leg, her supposed sewing job—well, it was a different use of needles that fascinated her. He remembered listening to a Polish woman, a devout Catholic, singing the song 'Californication'. She'd been lost in the beauty of the melody without realising the words ... What was beauty if you didn't know what lay behind it?

He hardly slept that night. She was grinding her teeth and he sweated under a series of fractured nightmares in which he could see beneath Alex's skin to a liquid pattern of red-plush and gold-veined flower.

Of course he would come back to Poland after Christmas and help her. But he was afraid. To come back to her would be like reviving a dying flower by setting it in water. He locked her in the flat when he went to work. Later Julian called round.

'I'm stressed. Put me to sleep, Liam,' he said, so Liam made him a big soporific joint. Feeding the habit. Injecting everyone. He'd given the tramp some money that morning which must have been spent on cheap alcohol. Being giving and sharing didn't make you a good person.

Their last afternoon together, he took Alex to the Irish pub. Let it stand, he had to tell her because she was impatient to try the Guinness. It was her first taste and she loved it, so he bought her a Guinness T-shirt. 'Irlandski super,' she said, doing the thumbs-up and kissing him. Then they had fun, bombing up and down the supermarket, throwing presents for his family in the trolley.

She hardly had anything to pack. The evening dragged and she tried to pierce her ear. She stuck a needle through it but became agitated because the earring was too big. There was blood everywhere. She phoned her Russian 'collega', colleagues as she called them, to buy amphetamines for her friend to take to her husband in prison the next day. Or so Liam understood, but what was the difference if he fully or half understood? They could only get it to her the following afternoon and she flung down the phone, biting her lips, inconsolable. Liam gave her six hundred zloty and drove to her friend's house in the country, where they had an emotional parting and he promised continually to come back for her. She shoved lots of the chocolates that he'd bought her back into his pockets. Her friend was going to try and help her get off heroin. The final wave goodbye ended with a great buzz of relief.

He got up early the next morning ready for the long drive. There were thumbprints of blood on the bathroom towel and half a sponge heart blackened with her hair dye.

He phoned his sister at the Polish/German border.

'I'll stop over in Holland tonight and be home late tomorrow.' He told her about Alex. 'I didn't use precautions. I'll have to get a test,' he said. His sister began to cry and he thought of Alex locked in the house in the country, the princess in the tower trusting him to come and save her. Forever. Epidermally yours. Tired, so tired. He had just passed border control but he pulled over onto the verge.

He hoped to God his blood was clear. And Alex's. He kicked at a decaying leaf, detaching it from the bare ground with which it was merging. He remembered that story about the Russians believing themselves resistant to death and he thought of Alex not throwing herself into life, but at it fearlessly. He'd wanted to look closely at a prostitute, lead the wild life while staying behind a cold observing screen but she'd chiselled her way through, file in hand. He laughed as it occurred to him that the Irish were descended from a race where immortals ran round with the mortals, were commingled. Maybe that was why he could be with Alex—all along she'd been looking to him to teach her about normal mortal life.

He was scarcely out of the country and he wanted to see her again.

It wasn't just a case of going round the world seeing things. It was about seeing things through.

The Door

AUTUMN'S EARLY UNDER THE TOASTED SKY, toasted leaves. My head's a rotting, spiked fruit. When I close my eyes I see a brain dissected and multicoloured, a mathematical model. Something lurid's there, inciting dreams of fantastical sex.

I have to wait before I rehydrate and detoxify, wait to be sure that the door from my room doesn't slam shut for no reason. I get up and make the mistake of glancing in the dresser mirror and the room stretches behind me, travelling. That was very careless; the last thing I wanted was to elongate the room, corridor it.

These crazy, zigzagging nights, getting into taxis, going places, going to Alcohol World. Everyone seems drunk. Well-dressed ladies stagger in unseemly style, a man falls out of a tram, a couple argue and split up, a man drunk punches another man. It is a drunk summer.

Dawn is a drink being poured; the sky has filled up with juice. In my room there are two reflections cast from the window. The first is the blurred, swaying, yellow-green leaves and blue sky living brightly on the sheened polish of the brown wardrobe. The other, squeezing through the open doorway of my room and finally resting on the front door, is smaller, paler, less defined; a reflection in a lake at dusk. And I wave and see the shadow of my hand waving back and in the smaller reflection my hand is no bigger than the antennaed head of an insect and it's possible that from the other flats someone can see me waving frantically for help.

I finally pluck up the courage to leave my room and go to the bathroom. Nothing happens, I'm allowed to go freely, and I breathe deep, my hands softening on the smooth shell of the sink, while the tree pipes and the waterfall taps cheer loudly. I tell myself to keep calm. Insanity is imagination. It's a vice, no different from cigarettes or beer.

It's about nine at night when I find it safe to leave my flat. On the landing, there's an old woman withdrawing backwards, slowly, into her doorway, all the time watching like a spider or a crab that makes a door out of its horny exterior. She has a black, oval-gemmed ring like a cockroach perched on her hand.

Downstairs the walls are shedding paint scales and their shabbiness is touching. In contrast, the walls of my flat are fresh-painted and pristine and the thin epidermis barely conceals a brittle resentment.

By the time I arrived, the party was up in motion, the atmosphere plump with fun, and I plunged into the big bowl of punch. It was a giant soporific, looking like the holy waters of health, a silver chalice on a white tablecloth.

The cause d'être of the party was the hostess' birthday and there was a bit of confusion as they sang the Wedding March first. It wasn't her flat but her parents'. Her boyfriend said she'd killed them and she laughed.

We made a toast: 'Let's all drink, so we don't forget how to!'

The balcony was lit up with candles in red glasses. In the distance, the moon was a washed up gemstone on the shore sky. I was discussing double identity with someone who said his childhood fear was that an identical child would come and take his place one day. I told him it wasn't unusual and I'd had an alter ego as a child but it had been a boy self and we'd switched bodies when we'd wanted.

Up above the cloud trees were echoing the trees below. The

hostess tried to get past me. Her breast touched me, flowers waving up her dress, the hot heads colliding, sprinkling me with pollen.

'Are you holding Tom's hand?' she smiled.

I glanced down. Apparently I was. An ill-judged move but natural. It felt like I was holding the hand of my boy-self.

The smoke rose from a cigarette like a tubular fugue, a cornucopia of a transparent lily. In the living room a tangle-legged insect was performing miraculous leaps and zigzagging thoughts under the light of a lamp. It was a brown sun worshipper under a sunbed, oblivious to the clicks and zips and revolutions of its own immolation.

Music was pumping in a vein through the joints of the flat and I went inside to feel it. A man had been left by his girlfriend to dance on his own. 'She's gone!' he cried tragically. 'Do you want that door?' his friend asked. Yes, he said, so the two men took the door off its hinges and began dancing with it between them. Inside the wooden frame was a rectangle of glass and they pressed themselves up against it like two thwarted lovers and they touched the outline of each other's body and squashed their lips against the hard membrane.

Just for a second, my heart caught on a thought-thread, a tripwire of belief, and I wondered if they could break through. Just for a second, then I started laughing again.

The whispers of danger were spreading. The bubbling saliva-surface of the punch looked like frog spit. The seething fruit tongues were alive and rolling in acid. Somebody found the antidote to the debilitating fermentation and prepared it—fresh coffee.

At that morning smell of coffee, a group of us fled into the aphelion, the darkest point of night, keeping our backs to the east. We took a taxi to the underpass, trawling exits for a non-stop bar under hot, low, murky strip lighting. There were holes in the roof where empty cans had been thrown. Nowhere was sealed, nowhere was stoppered.

As we come out, the sun is licking the rim of the clouds. Above the web of the intersection of trams, an airplane trail is lit up like the path of a moth that's caught the sun and flown on burning.

A lake of liquid gold has burst its dam and is spreading in the middle of the road. The black trams, coming from night, slide on the vitreous candescence. An old lady outside the church gates picks up a plastic bag and puts it in her bag. She has eyebrows of wild grey seam-stitches stitched by a mad seamstress and there are dark flocked wings on her forehead. She hangs her bag on the railings of the gate and takes out what I first think is a key. She kisses it and clasps it to her chest, branding herself with its gold, hoping it can burn into her soul. As she kisses the crucifix, she starts to chew each of the four points, then eats and devours it, her lips becoming full of juice, no longer retracted with age.

She shakes the gate but it's locked.

This city of light, a gigantic, glimmering firefly nestled in the earth. I know I've left it late. I jingle the key in the lock of my flat. It takes an hour before the door opens like a wakening eyelid. The sleepy bed stares at me sullenly. The mouths of the drawers are tight and grim and I'm tired of the secret looks and winks of the cabal around me.

I snuggle quietly under the bedclothes and sleep comes, its steel spoon scooping my thoughts out, leaving a pithy, sweet skin.

When finally I wake, I rub my eyes, two bruises on a peach skin, and take the first greedy suck of the new day. I take in my surroundings, sustaining with half-closed eyes the powerful onslaught of a horrible discovery: I'm distraught. Sorry, I whisper, sorry. Because the door has gone. The two sides of the wall have grafted over where the door used to be. It is perfect craftmanship, not a crack or a crease or a suture or seam. It's as though there was never a door and I grew in here gradually, like a crystal culture.

I'm on the eighth floor. There's no exit. I want to scream at this immurement. I shouldn't have come back. I should have left the place when the trouble first started.

I scan the walls. The mirror. Maybe I could dive into the mercury river of the mirror. I wistfully eye the painting of children playing at the mill, looking high and low and in every dimension for the antidote, the dark antibodies. An idea, like a feather fast-spinning vertically down from the heavens, lands in my grasp. My boy-self. My boy-self is somewhere else. I'll swap minds. He can die here in my place because he never existed anyway.

I'm scared. It's been so long. Can I go back to being a child? I feel cruel, guilty. Killing products of your imagination, let alone your half-self, is still murder, recognisable in any court of the land.

I'm on the point of giving up when the sun suddenly strengthens. The light, filtered through the trees outside, comes in through the window and casts breathing scales on the wall where the door once was. The web-thin scrapes in the old windowpane are magnified in long veil-strips of white. I step towards the wall-screen of light and my shadow gets taller, lengthens. The light splashes its soft, warm rain on my back, and it's like walking through a lace curtain blowing in the breeze.

I've noticed, in recent months, events beginning to hide away, wilting with inadequacy under hopeful expectations, under the pressure of being committed to paper, and I feel like giving up on things ever happening. But it's important to remember that there is still time.

I fill my hours with walks, some linear, some circular and, just to vary it, some rectangular and sometimes wild rhombi or even decahedrons. In fact, I've followed every possible course in the gamut of many-planed configurations—up steps and down slopes, threading out shapes twisted and mutated beyond recognition, beyond the permitted laws of variation. When asked where I was going, I would always reply, 'Back.'

On occasion on these walks, I've stumbled into cemeteries, following the criss-cross paths, burying myself in the maze. On certain days, I stop to observe the priest waving his cross over the mourners and I look up and wonder how many miles it is to Heaven. Two thousand two hundred miles? The reality of the grave is disappointing but from where I stand it's like paradise watching the families waiting, so quiet, solemn and unworldly. They catch my eye and they look through me as if I'm transparent, a passionless ghost peering out from the inside of a half-eaten cave, from the hollowed-out cadaver of life. As the priest leaves, slapping the dust from his knees, the motorised cart that bore the coffin races away, churning up dust in its wake. The dust is thick-lying, ground by a pestle from the mortar of the earth, and the mourners faint under the pipette of the sun's rays. Like a beach, the ridged roots of the trees become sand-covered tide marks and the dead, like sunbathers lazing in enchanted vacuity, look up to the sky. And I lie down on a bench and dream of staying there for ever. But the important thing is that there is still time.

It was today that I threw out my diary. Just as I reached the skip, about to offer up the diary, I saw a silver-scaled snake, coiling and slithering among the rubbish and I jumped. Another flash of movement revealed to me a woman standing on the other side of the skip, poking a stick into the detritus, looking for treasures. She had spotted a silver shower hose and was trying to lift it with her stick.

From a flat high up in the clouds someone was shouting, 'Maman.' The newly cut grass smelled of white wine and I chucked my diary on the pyre of rubbish.

I decided to get out of my quarter. Outside the building, some men were leaning forward on the bench like some great spectacle was unfolding in front of them. Hooked to the air was a walking stick and they chattered excitedly and smoked from cheap, paper packets.

I took the bus to the market. On the way there, the trees clouded up and steamed, their anger unleashed by the darkening wind and, as I arrived, I had to take shelter under an awning of orange sacks as the first giant drops of rain fell. The open air sellers rushed around trying to cover their goods which were laid on sheets in the grass square. Some just sat, rolling a grey, hooded eye up to the sky, and swigging from bottles wrapped in newspaper. In the flicking fingers of the wind the pigeons swelled out like burst pillows. I saw a pair of dusty, mile-worn shoes blacken in the rain. Each drop fell hard, splattering its core, spilling tiny lodestars of wet. A fur monkey was quickly bundled into a waterproof mac. Rain fell like stones down a well into china cups and bowls. Carpets changed to the colour of moss or mulched bracken round a small pool. A husband was late to return and his wife, beads of purified rage flying from her hair, screamed at him with doubling, trebling ferocity, pointing at the water-washed paintings, the worlds therein utterly sea-changed.

The clouds developed tiny splits and light rays finally pierced them with their weight and poured forth like white waterfalls. The storm was over and damp lace curtains were let loose into the air and all clothing unfurled to shake off the clinging damp; everywhere was a riot of celebratory flags. I walked along a path through the market and it was strewn with puddles and cabbage leaves like the shallowest of lily ponds. Vegetables and fruit were as bright and smooth as pebbles washed up on the shore.

I called in at the fishmonger's to visit the carp. Black rocks with orange-moustached mouths moved their gills slowly in the bubbling tub. They pouted hello back at me and blew kisses. I walked down the row of bouquet sellers—those old wizened women were lined up like grinning bridesmaids in a photograph. The most fetching of them held a funeral bouquet close to her breast.

The tide of the storm had carried leaves and flowers onto the pavement and a man was sweeping them to one side with a birch broomstick; it was as if he was wielding a great paddle as he floated down the grey path. He'd built up a small mound on the edge of the market and, as I left, I looked across at the cold mud of reality and it made me shiver.

On the way back to my bus stop, I noticed something strange: there were smiles on people's faces—not of sudden laughter but of the joke that had passed along the street—the light from their eyes rebounding with pleasure, wanting everyone to share. Straight ahead I caught sight of a joyous red jumper. Its wearer had a tweed cap, a big leather bag on his back and walked with a steel crutch. A puppy was trotting beside him. I caught up with them as the man stopped and collected his wine in a plastic bag from a friend at the crossroads. This man of about fifty had an aged, driftwood face buffeted by life's storms. There were soft rain-marks in the sands of his skin and curling wrinkles round his eyes. He had an amber-coloured beard, as though the red of his lips had rusted. At the heel of his boots, worn down like smooth black pebbles, the tiniest puppy capered. The puppy was barking deliriously at his master's steel crutch, hoping that the impudent silver stick would snap back at him, thereby necessitating a swift bite of retaliation. The man played along, stomping his stick on the ground.

Suddenly, the puppy spied a plastic bag puffed up like a conch in the gutter and saw the opportunity of work to be done. He lifted it with his teeth and carried it along, a little version of his master, big paws held high as if walking through deep puddles. Soon the puppy tired of his burden. The rainburst had unstoppered the fragrances around and the puppy veered away to investigate. The vendors picked him up and kissed him, letting him anoint their fingers and faces with his wriggling tongue before leaving them to scamper back.

Divine shafts of light from the lifting sky played around them as they walked. Even in the hardest mind, the humour that was crouched in some recess, slowly unhunched, stood upright and leapt out in unfettered laughter and smiles reflected like shining mirrors held high along the street. And I joined this joyful entourage, walking just a few yards away, and the man smiled at me from under his jagged antler brows. I caught sight of his eyes and within the fleshy petals was a startling blue light, a drop of dew nestling in a vale of tears.

A vendor, some Russian gangster in a black fedora, was lounging back in a deckchair, throwing sweets into his mouth, the candy coats clinking off his hard teeth. He smacked his lips and offered a sweet seeded in the depth of his hand but the heady mixture of old coins and sweetness was too much and the puppy turned tail in confusion. Confidence regained, he swaggered towards some men drinking cans, liking their rowdiness.

'Market!' called the man and the puppy raced back.

I'd followed this happy heart procession for a long way when they arrived at a tram stop. I leant against the railing, keeping a distance of some yards. The man stroked his tangled thicket of beard and checked the tram numbers, then lit a cigarette. He held it in his fingers like he was playing a small whistle, fingers poised. Two women asked him questions about the puppy and I watched, as he spoke, the blue flower-eyes, sprung from wells of moisture, blooming in the dry brown desert of his face. He graced me with another of his curving-cheekbone smiles and I could see the countryside in his soft-grained, swirling wrinkles follow meandering paths, not hard horizontals. His face had the gentle gnaw of time, unmarred by deep hacks with the axe, and goodness had been harvested in the temperate swathes.

The puppy watched cars go past with pricked-back ears, showing no fear. He sketched their rhythm with his snail-shell eyes, flecked and oiled and inquisitive.

The tram pulled in and I took one of the seats behind them. The man held the puppy in his arms. His fingers, broadened by heavy work, were much wider than the puppy's legs. I felt shy. I didn't want them to think I was a mad person tracking them, but I couldn't just let them go. I wanted to see where they lived, so I'd know one secret place of love in the world. Moreover, though it wasn't logical, I had a feeling that this time I wasn't on a walk that returns to the start.

We went deep into the old industrial heart of the city, rattling up the vital vein into the aortic chamber, the region where the workers slept, the roads narrowing and turning, the tram lines running over old cobblestones on a bumpy, clotted ride.

It was in a part of the city I didn't know existed that the old man and the puppy got off the tram. I was relieved when they didn't look round and, this time, I stayed a respectable distance behind them. The streets were quiet here but the puppy still threw out his magic lure and a small child ran over like a full-breasted, splay-footed bird and lavished on him her ardent, ham-fisted hugs. I stood in a doorway, out of view.

We passed a row of murky, brown-painted shops with striped awnings. It was hard to think of them as living businesses. Outside the bakery, the puppy stopped to sniff at the fresh smell of newborn bread, then zigzagged after the man in a zany, undecided spree, like an overgrown bumblebee drawn everywhere by the multiple summer scents.

The street widened briefly and high brick walls stretched along the left side, to the world like a prison. Through a gate with swirling metal arabesques, luxuriant giant daisies peeped out, the most delicate of filigrees noosing them round the neck. I witnessed an odd sensation, as much a feeling as a vision. It was hot summer and understandably the man was breathing pulsatingly, pulling at the oxygen, his whole body heaving with the effort. And I looked up, drawn by the breeze high in the treetops flourishing over the cemetery walls and suddenly I saw the green leaves sucking at the oxygen, too, beginning to stir and breathe, the branches beating like veins in a lung, the great organism of plant life echoing one man.

They turned left down an adjoining street and I followed quickly, anxious not to lose them. Just in time. The man was in the doorway of a building. The puppy in one last flurry of freedom charged at the doves eating sunflower seeds on the pavement and they flew up like five-tipped stars, fluttering and fanning out their tail wings. Through the starry commotion of wings, the man met my eyes and a smile sparked in his dark woodgrain face.

'Market,' he called and the door closed behind them.

They were gone. One tiny click of metal was all it took. That was the ultimate power of all doors, to come between people. I went to examine the list of names by the buzzer. There were only strips of white, empty card. The building was crack-painted and badly weathered—it seemed as though worms had been burrowing within the pocked surfaces of the brick.

I tried the door handle. It opened. You could smell a damp like peat seeping into wood.

I wondered which flat was theirs. There was a choice of six. I listened outside the first door I came to. I was embarrassed by the extent of my neediness but I couldn't yet go home. I'd come too far and it wasn't ridiculous to establish where they lived. All I needed were a few sounds—a rush of paws, a clink of a bottle, a happy sigh—to take home for comfort, to throw into the unquiet, truculent waters of imagination and placate the unrest, for once.

On the upper floor, I heard a high-pitched mewing and scratching at a door. It sounded urgent. I pushed aside the doubts and twisted the handle. The door opened. I could see straight through into the bedroom where the man was lying open-eyed on a bulky bed made up of overcoats. His right arm was hanging down as if he were lying in a boat on a summer day, running his fingers through the water.

I ran over to him. His open eyes were unflinching and I took hold of his wrist, squeezing it tightly. I couldn't detect even the faintest beat but in my own wrist I felt a large pulsing. I saw it swell, vibrate, and I stared helplessly as the skin struggled and writhed and, hatching out of pure terror, a winged insect began to flap inside my vein, lashing and frothing up the blood and the torrent exploded up my arm and my head screamed with fear, as it plunged into black.

I flittered in and out of a tenebrous consciousness, aware of drifting and floating to another place, attended by a cortège of unknown voices. It took me a long time to waken fully and realise I was in a bed that wasn't mine. I was in a light, airy, private room of a hospital. I lay still, trying to piece back the past into a semblance of sense.

The key in a lock turned and a doctor entered the room.

'How are you?'

'Fine, I think.'

'Can you remember what happened?'

I told him about the man and the puppy. I was very concerned for the fate of them both.

The doctor looked at me with an intense fervour.

'Laura,' he said and I didn't like him using my name. How could he have developed a bond with a body that was lying unconscious? Five minutes ago he would have called me 'her' or 'the woman'. Now he was calling me Laura.

'Laura, you must guard against letting dreams slip into reality through cracks and fissures. You have to plaster even the tiniest fracture in your memory in order to be whole again.'

'I am whole!' I protested.

He explained to me how easy it was to implant memories of childhood events into a mind. It's usual that later in life you are told by your parents what happened to you as a child, so you assimilate the experience by simple image-making and insert it into the mindfill, creating a history as authentic or inauthentic as dreams themselves, not a brainwash but a cerebral regeneration—a brainpolish, honing past times to beautiful perfection.

I could accept this. I could accept that the crystallised image of crystal fairy lights which I'd gazed at from my bed as a small child was in fact a transference from my mother's memory. But it was preposterous to think that the man and the puppy were a falsely implanted dream.

'Where was I found?' I asked.

'In a squat in the west of the city,' he said, confirming what I knew to be true, but he quickly added, 'Neighbours heard cries. No one else was there.'

'Can I go?'

'I'm sorry. You're a risk to yourself.'

The doctor pointed at my wrist. It was wrapped in thin gauze which I plucked to one side, revealing a pink rend in the skin, a snow-capped rivulet of faded pain.

I looked into his eyes and he transposed in me the smallest memory of doubt. I had a feeling that this time I wasn't on a walk that returns to the start.

'Take some water,' he said, pouring me a glass. 'With this.'

'This' was a lurid-coloured pill, a tiny larva of trouble, that could metamorphose, transmogrify the taker into any state the creator so designed.

'I never take pills. Not even for headaches,' I replied.

He was insistent, so I demolished it with my teeth and spat out the chalky fragments.

'Okay, I've taken it. Happy, now?' I asked.

He stalked out angrily and I knew he'd be back soon.

I could see in the depths of the ridged water bottle, glass steps leading up into a spiral. I grabbed the bottle and tilted it back, drinking deep from the opaque throat of life. It was all finished and it was only just starting.

I left my bed and padded over in the soft white slippers, treading on cotton clouds, to the window. There was a shrouded angel lying in the sky. You could make out the thin rays of its ribs and the parabola of its backbone and its long, emaciated fingers, gathering in the folds of the gossamer shroud. It was reclining on slopes of descending pink and all the colour was gradually being sucked into the hole that the sun had left; the weight of heavy blue was pushing the pink ever downward.

The fragility of the beauty made me want to cry for the ultimate doom of the earth and at the same time, I was ecstatically happy to be still breathing from the bowl of ephemeral colours and I broke into laughter. With a sigh of relief, my mind settled. In exchange for taking the tablets, I'd make one request of the doctor. To protect my mind against the assault of extraneous abstracts, essences or solids, I wished to keep a diary.

The Flame

EVERY JUNE IN POLAND'S LAKE DISTRICT there were many incidents of drownings, accompanied by weather that could only be described as phenomenal. The storms had the strength to wrench boats off their moorings, capsize them and then were gone in a whisper.

The village of Mikowaiki stretched out between the shoreline and forest in a narrow cluster of white houses and the lake itself was a smooth, reflective petal of light, studded with shimmering-sailed yachts, an archipelago of tiny, moving islands. Walking through the village, you could smell the opaline sweetness of strawberries in the air and from shopfronts, you were greeted by winking half-oranges and grinning slices of watermelon. Old men and women sat on walls, fanning themselves with leaves, and there seemed to be a surfeit of peace and time here that could never be exhausted or squandered.

Anna had arrived late in the afternoon. It hadn't taken her long to find a *pension* as it was only June and the lakes weren't in high season. She freshened up, then wandered down to the village.

She took a seat on the top balcony of a bar, overlooking the water's edge. In the distance she could see the roofs of chalets signalling through the trees like heaven-turned arrow tips. The posthumous smoke from afternoon grills slowly revolved in rays of sunlight. For a second, she felt emptiness inside, a small cave of loneliness, for she was travelling alone round Poland, but then the irresistible beauty of the sunset filled the cavern and she forgot everything.

The moon, a cuticle of white ice, slowly materialised. The sky and even the whitest building turned dove pink and the sunburnt faces and shoulders of the passers-by glowed pinkly. An after-sun fever made them shiver with cold numbness and the air began to speckle with dusky swarms of mosquitoes.

The bar was getting full and a group of friends from Warsaw joined Anna's table. They were already drunk and raucous. One man who could scarcely speak a word of English held court to the others by trying to converse with Anna.

'What is London in English?' he asked and everybody roared.

It became too dark on the balcony, so they moved down to the beer garden, inviting Anna to join them. The day was bruising into night. The men and women walking along the path were wearing grey-blue eye shadow and blusher, made up by the night and moon powder. Blades of light flashed on the women's collarbones.

A bottle of tequila was passed round the table. They made rowdy toasts, clinking their glasses.

Anna was lighting a cigarette from the candle when she felt someone standing over her, blocking out the light, and was compelled to look.

'Don't you know,' demanded the stranger, 'that when you light a cigarette with a candle, somewhere a sailor dies?'

The table fell quiet. Anna was transfixed by the deep purple eyes full of anger. The man had a grotesque, key-shaped scar scored into his forehead and another silvery scar down his pale cheek, the white cutting through his lip.

'Can't you see what you have done?' the man upbraided her again.

Without warning, he plucked the cigarette from between her fingers and threw it into her glass of beer where it briefly hissed on impact, then swayed and sank to the bottom. Anna stared in shock as he turned and marched away, the long, oilskin coat beating against his legs. The white of his face turned bronze as he disappeared into first the dark blue iris of the night, then into its inky pupil.

The table gradually recovered its buoyant humour.

'It's only an old Polish superstition,' said someone.

'Don't worry about that crazy man,' added one girl. 'He likes to kill fun,' and she made a chopping motion with her hand into her neck.

Though she joked the whole episode off, the man's weirdness, his intense rage, still played on Anna's mind. She had to make a conscious effort to join in with the others.

'We're going to a different bar. Want to come?' the girl asked her.

'Sure,' she said.

They all left together. Anna was walking beside one of the men when he suddenly said, 'Excuse me, please,' and started running. He jumped into the back of the estate car into which the rest of the gang had piled. Some people waved at her and the car crunched on a fast turn and sped off.

They'd ditched her; the second surprise of the night. Though she was hurt, it was probably just as well, since they were going a few kilometres from Mikowaiki and she hadn't even thought about how to get back alone. Yet, she knew that from the moment the man had extinguished her cigarette, they'd been uncomfortable with her presence, as if she were a bad talisman.

She decided to go home and walked back up the lake path, stepping carefully over the snares of ropes. Emanating from the lake was an acrid smell, almost molten as if one of the stars from above had fallen in. Out of the corner of her eye, she spotted a churning motion, some sharded light, in the water, but when she paused to look, it was as quiet and reflective as lacquered wood. In the trees, a secret rustling sound could be heard, followed by a nervous whistle of wings. Anna pulled her jacket closer round her chest.

She left the lakeside and went through the village, following the road up into the outskirts. She couldn't believe how few electric lights there were. And more darkness was gathering as the moon and stars were blown out one by one by a strengthening wind and a dense cloud was drawn from the rim of the horizon across the sky.

Anna stopped. She couldn't recognise the street. It had been perfectly simple to walk down from her *pension* to the lake, but her senses now were blurred from drink. The jagged-backed snake of dark trees lying in the fields twisted suddenly and she was scared, at last realising the folly of walking alone in a deserted area she didn't know. She recalled the man in the pub and was now certain that he or someone was watching her, though her mind told her instincts to be calm and not to be so stupid as to fall prey to a backdrop of creeping superstition.

She speeded up her step, looking for a house, a tree, a gate she recognised—anything. She could hear dogs howling in the distance and a greater howling rose from within the bodies of the trees as the wind fluted through the hollows. She looked down and an icy punch of fear exploded inside her. A small, red light was following her steps. She stopped and checked the street behind her, looking for shadows behind cars, faces at open chinks in curtains, but there was no one. She swallowed hard but the backwash of fear slewed up in her throat and the rhythm of her heart began to beat in her ears. She walked on and again she lowered her gaze and saw the light, inches in front, and the noise in her head drummed louder and louder as she looked around, this way and that, turning, wheeling …

Emerging from a shadow under a streetlight was a figure in a dark, hooded coat. And in its hand, swinging back and forth, a light washed in a blood red.

She ran blindly to the end of the street, and saw that there was nowhere to go, a dead end leading into dark, grass pools and trees that were cowering, hunching and lashing back at the wind. Without looking behind, she plunged into the trees, their paroxysmal convulsions of pain and agony and beating of their breasts blotting out the thud in her head and, in all the clamour, she went flying down, finally hitting the water with a smack, her head going under, then hurtling up, shaking and gasping. She was conscious of being in a stream, slow moving, stagnant, and she felt a sudden warmth on the side of her cheek and turned, and the last thing she saw was the red as a hand closed round her neck, pushing her down into the choking waters.

The storm gripped the resort harder. Out on the lake, a yacht, on which a teenage boy had been sleeping, was being relentlessly battered by the waves.

A man was watching from under the gusting eaves of the trees. The boy, hurled this way and that in the mouth of the storm, let out a long scream. As the boat tipped over, the man tore off his coat and flung himself into the lake. By the time he'd battled against the high waves to the boat's edge, the boy had disappeared. He dived under and managed to clutch the body and haul it up from the greedily sucking water. A dozen times the chopping waves tried to free the body but the man clung on and pulled it back to the shore.

He dragged the inert body onto the path and knelt over it, pushing back the tangle of wet hair. A stream of water trickled from its lips as from the neck of a sculpted bowl. The blanched, delicate face wasn't that of a boy. It was Anna.

Anna's eyes shot open. As the blood pumped into her brain, a rope of images unwound before her: a boat rocking violently in the sea, a sailor smashing headfirst against the wheelhouse and the blood splattering onto the hot glass of the lantern ... She watched a body float ashore and, as it was turned, face up, she cried out, recognising the scars. A coffin was lowered into the ground in a quiet summer graveyard overlooking the lake. She plunged below the soil and, in a moment of pure torment, was trapped beside this man beating against the coffin lid. She tried to quieten him, reaching to restrain his arms, but the damp body lay motionless and she shuddered, realising it was his fury, a distilled force, that was wreaking the madness. She suddenly understood that he'd been brought home against his will.

'I told you,' crept a whisper. 'Use the light from a candle and you will kill a sailor.'

She sat up. The man was already walking away along the path. He raised the light to the tip of his cigarette and, as the smoke filtered from his scarred lips, he slowly dispersed in a coil of white.

Anna turned. In terror, she saw the upturned boat bobbing in the still lake.